Missing Persons

Books by Michael Brandman

The Jesse Stone Novels
Robert B. Parker's Killing the Blues
Robert B. Parker's Fool Me Twice
Robert B. Parker's Damned If You Do

Other Novels
Missing Persons

Missing Persons

Michael Brandman

Poisoned Pen Press

Copyright © 2017 by Michael Brandman

First Edition 2017

10 9 8 7 6 5 4 3 2 1

Library of Congress Catalog Card Number: 2017934130

ISBN: 9781464208041   Hardcover
      9781464208065   Trade Paperback

Poisoned Pen Press
4014 N. Goldwater Boulevard, #201
Scottsdale, Arizona 85251
www.poisonedpenpress.com
info@poisonedpenpress.com

Printed in the United States of America

For Joanna…
…with my love and gratitude for the
amazing first forty years…

"The iniquities of the Father shall be visited upon the sons."
—*Deuteronomy*

"Or not."
—*Burton Steel, Junior*

Chapter One

A scorching heat wave blanketed the West Coast, bringing with it record temperatures, rolling blackouts, and a general feeling of malaise that infected everyone.

A fast-moving Mexican monsoon, however, was now gaining strength in the Gulf of Mexico, steaming up the California coast accompanied by gale force winds and heavy rain.

It would most likely reach Freedom by late afternoon. I sat staring out the office window, elated that the storm would finally end the stultifying heat, but also apprehensive of the possible havoc it might wreak.

"Global warming," I thought.

A late model green Toyota Camry pulled up in front of the San Remo County Courthouse. I watched as a middle-aged woman emerged, looked around, then headed inside.

After a few moments, I heard Sheriff's Deputy Johnny Kennerly talking with the woman. Then he appeared in my doorway and stood there, fanning himself with a legal size yellow pad.

"There's a Rosalita Gonzalez here to see you."

I swiveled my chair around to face him. "What about?"

"You mean what does she want?"

"Yes."

"She wants to see you."

"So you said. What does she want to see me about?"

"I didn't ask."

"You didn't ask?"

"I'm a Deputy Sheriff, not a personal assistant."

"You had me fooled. I guess that means a donut run is out."

Johnny fanned himself faster. "Funny," he said.

I soldiered on. "So you don't know why she's here."

"Correct."

"Do you find that at all strange?"

"No."

"I find it strange."

"And I should care about that because?"

I gave him my best dead-eyed stare.

"Would you like me to show her in?" Johnny asked.

"Only if it meshes with your job description."

Johnny stopped fanning himself and grinned. "I'll have to check my contract."

He went to get Rosalita Gonzalez, who followed him into my office. She looked to be in her fifties, gray-haired, wearing a tight green summer shift that had once fit her better. She lowered her brow and eyed the surroundings, clearly uncomfortable.

I stood and offered her a seat. "If you're not too busy, Deputy Kennerly, would you please join us?"

Johnny nodded. He was a big man, six-foot-six, dark-skinned with large brown eyes and a wide mouth—features he had inherited from his African American father. His Romanesque nose was a duplicate of his Italian mother's. He wore a khaki Sheriff's Department uniform with a handful of service badges pinned to his shirt. A .357 magnum was holstered on his hip.

"How may we help you, Ms. Gonzalez?" I sat down and smiled, encouraging her to speak.

She got right to it. "Have you ever heard of Barry Long, Junior?"

"Who hasn't?"

"I work for him. I'm nanny to his son."

"Okay."

"There's something wrong."

"Meaning?"

"Mrs. Long has disappeared." She looked quickly at both of us, trying to gauge our response. "Sometime last week."

I glanced at Johnny who was seated beside Ms. Gonzalez. He had a quizzical look in his eye.

"Reverend Long," she continued, "told me she had gone away for a while. He said I was to take full charge of the boy."

"Did he mention where she had gone?"

"No."

"What exactly did he say?"

"What he didn't say was when she would come back."

"How old is the boy?"

"Barely five. He's very upset. Very unhappy. The Reverend is preparing for his annual revival Celebration and he moves back and forth between the house and his apartment at the Pavilion. Now he takes me and the boy with him. The boy cries and carries on a lot. He's always screaming for his mother. When I try to talk about it with the Reverend, he tells me to handle it."

"What is it you want from the Sheriff's Department?"

"Reverend Long, he scares me."

She cleared her throat and went on. "He and the men around him. They're not good people. There's something wrong there."

"And you want us to look into it?"

"I want you to know what's going on. What you do is up to you. I can't be a part of it anymore. I'm leaving."

"You mean you're quitting?"

"I mean I'm leaving. I'm going somewhere to hide and pray they never find me."

She stood and stared at me and at Johnny for several moments before picking up her purse and walking to the door.

Then she turned back to us.

"I think they killed her."

Chapter Two

Freedom wasn't the future I had in mind for myself. At age thirty, I had been faring quite well as a ranking LAPD homicide detective. I stand six-three in my bare feet, a former point guard, weighing in at one-seventy. I have blue eyes and dark blond hair, which I tend to haphazardly.

I worked out of the Hollywood division and lived within walking distance of the Cole Avenue Station. I was unmarried, with a promising career in law enforcement that impressed at least some of the women at my fitness club who believed, as did I, that hooking up was a satisfactory alternative to commitment. I was feeling as if I'd arrived, for whatever that was worth.

Then my father took ill. He hadn't felt well during his re-election campaign and once he claimed victory, he paid a much-delayed visit to his GP.

He was quietly admitted to a private clinic where he underwent a battery of tests. One of the state's leading neurologists consulted on the findings and confirmed the initial diagnosis of Amyotrophic Lateral Sclerosis, otherwise known as Lou Gehrig's disease.

For the popular Sheriff of San Remo County—a coastal area located north of Santa Barbara—about to begin his third consecutive four-year term, this finding was nothing short of catastrophic.

He summoned the family. My sister flew in from Chicago. I drove up from L.A. Our stepmother, Regina Goodnow, herself the estimable mayor of Freedom Township, fluttered about the house doing all she could to ease the tension and make us comfortable.

My father, Burton Steel, Senior, was uncharacteristically subdued, his oversized personality deflated by the collapse of his heretofore robust health.

I'm Burton Steel, Junior. I hate the name Burton. I dislike the Junior part even more. Naming me after himself, in my estimation, was the ultimate in Burton Senior's egocentricity, one of his innumerable character flaws. To differentiate us, I'm called Buddy.

My relationship with my father is complicated. I can't say we're friends. He's autocratic to a fault and I could hardly wait to graduate from high school and get the hell out of his house.

I fled my life in Freedom and moved to New York where I studied criminal justice at John Jay College. I graduated near the top of my class, and when the offer to join the LAPD popped up, I grabbed it.

Now the family was gathered in the living room of the home I grew up in, an English-style manor house located in the hills above Highway 101.

When the old man broke the news, he spoke haltingly, already exhibiting the effects of the disease on his vocal cords, his voice rough as gravel, and suffering a loss of velocity.

"I've been given a death sentence. I've got fucking Lou Gehrig's disease."

My sister, Sandra, gasped.

"It's in its early stages," he went on. "But I'm a goner, sure as shit."

Her Honor, my stepmother, chimed in. "Burton, please watch your language. You know how much I dislike all this swearing."

"Shut up, Regina."

"What can they do for it?" I pulled myself back from imagining the worst, hoping instead to hear some kind of optimistic prognosis.

"There's no cure. They've put me on steroids. Prednisone. I can already feel the difference."

"You mean you feel better?"

"I feel worse. Steroids slam the weight on you. It won't be long before I look like fucking Oprah."

"Burton, please," Regina snapped.

Sandra leaned forward. "Is there anything we can do?"

My father shifted his eyes to fix his stare directly at me.

"I need you, Buddy. I'm likely to fade pretty fast. I want you here as my chief deputy. I'll teach you the ropes. Train you to succeed me."

"You're kidding," I said, but I knew better.

Chapter Three

"So, what do we know about Barry Long, Junior?"

I was in the squad room, huddling with Johnny Kennerly and Captain Marsha Russo.

The three of us were seated at Marsha's desk. She and Johnny were in full regalia, their milk-chocolate-colored Sheriff's uniforms clean and sharply pressed.

I, on the other hand, was casually dressed. Blue jeans, plaid work shirt, a cream-colored corduroy jacket, and Filson work boots comprised my wardrobe of choice. As was the case with my time in the LAPD, I was a plainclothes guy, preferring to conceal my position as a law enforcement officer and producing another bone of contention between my father and me.

Marsha was focused on her computer, scouring websites until she found what she was looking for and then proceeded to read aloud.

She was a formidable woman, strong-willed and feisty, in her early forties, a veteran of fifteen years with the department. She pre-dated my father, and when he appointed Johnny Kennerly as Undersheriff, he'd asked her to join the command unit as a staff Captain.

She was short and thickset, forever fighting a battle with the scale. She had once been considered cute, but age and stress had taken their toll. Her trenchant wit and sharp tongue kept people on their toes.

"Here it is," she said. "Barry Long, Junior. Born March 6th, 1984, LaGrange, Tennessee. Father: Barry Long, Senior. Mother: Selma Hickham Long, deceased. Brother: Hickham Long. Sister: Margaret Long. No other siblings."

"Go on."

"Graduated LaGrange High School, class of 2002. Graduated South Tennessee Seminary College, class of 2006. Performed missionary services in Montevideo, Uruguay, 2007. Founded the Heart of Our Saviour Ministry in 2008."

"When did he go on TV?"

"His first broadcast was July 4th, 2010, on WTWV in Memphis, a Christian broadcasting service. They still carry him, by the way."

Marsha continued to scroll and read aloud:

"The Long Ministry television broadcasts are currently seen in fifteen countries. They are reputed to gross more than twenty-million dollars annually. The Heart of Our Saviour revival Celebration is held every year during the first week of October and televised in those same fifteen countries."

"Is there any mention of a Mrs. Long?"

"There is. Mary Catharine Morecombe Long. Born: July 2nd, 1994, Memphis, Tennessee. Married Barry Long, Junior, June 29th, 2012. One child, Barry Long, the third. Born: November 20, 2012."

"Which means she was pregnant when they got married," I interjected.

"And she was eighteen years old," Johnny added.

"That's a ten-year difference in their ages," I said. "When did they move to Freedom?"

"It doesn't say."

"Check the real estate records."

Marsha clicked onto a different site.

"They live in the old Schuyler estate," Johnny said.

"I found it," Marsha said. "The Horace B. Schuyler estate in San Remo County was sold to the Barry and Catharine Long Family Trust on September 14th, 2012, for a purchase price of three million, five hundred thousand dollars. Wow."

"Wow, indeed. Have you ever seen the Schuyler estate?"

Johnny shook his head.

"I hear it's amazing," Marsha said.

"Shall we?"

"Shall we what?"

"Have a look."

"You mean actually visit the Schuyler house?"

"It's the Long house now."

Johnny watched as I picked up my pad and pencil and stood. "If we leave now, we can beat the rain."

Chapter Four

The Long house sat on sixty acres of prime oceanfront property, separated from the sea by ten-plus acres of federally protected sand dunes.

The imposing mansion maintained its original nineteenth-century facade, despite the fact that it had been upgraded and modernized on several occasions over the years. Newly added floor-to-ceiling picture windows looked out onto the bay and the Pacific beyond. Its magnificent views remained impeded on the upper floors by sloping dormer windows that constricted the home's sight lines but maintained the architectural integrity of the original design.

After announcing myself at the call box in front of the estate's massive wrought-iron gates, I navigated the winding driveway that led to the rambling house. The grounds were immaculately tended. Rolling lawns were dotted with a variety of indigenous cacti and succulents. Acacia, palo verde, and live oak trees provided shade and character.

I parked in the circular motor court in front of the house beside a number of vans loaded with luggage and gear.

Johnny, Marsha, and I climbed the five steps to the wraparound front porch where we were greeted by a neatly groomed, efficient-looking young man dressed in a black suit, white shirt, black knit tie, and dark Ray-Ban sunglasses.

"Welcome to Long House."

The young man flashed a smile that revealed a mouthful of the largest and whitest teeth I had ever seen. I was mesmerized by them.

"How may we help you?" His smile reflected a forced sincerity.

"We'd like to see Mrs. Long."

The young man hesitated for a moment. "Mrs. Long isn't here."

"When do you expect her?"

"I'm not exactly sure."

"You're not sure."

"No," the young man said. "Mrs. Long is not in residence at this time."

"Do you know where she is?"

"I'm sorry, sir, I don't."

At that point, the door to the house opened and another man came out and headed in our direction. He was obviously a person of some importance.

"Hickham Long," the man announced, without offering his hand.

"Buddy Steel," I said. "This is John Kennerly and Marsha Russo."

Long acknowledged us. Then he turned to the young man. "That's all, Jeffrey. You can go."

Jeffrey looked at Hickham Long, then at me. He lowered his eyes and returned to the house.

"Now," Long said, "what can we do for you?"

"We're here to see Catharine Long," I said.

"I'm terribly sorry." Long shook his head. "My sister-in-law is away."

"Your sister-in-law."

"That's right. Reverend Long is my brother."

"I see. I'd still like to ask her a few questions. Have you any idea as to how we might contact her?"

Long shook his head again. "Not a clue."

He struck me as a disagreeable type, exhibiting no discernible warmth and exuding a general attitude of impatience, condescension, and imperiousness.

He was stocky, muscle-bound, possessing a physique molded by hours in the gym, mean-looking and sullen. His dense black hair was slicked back with pomade, rendering it strangely immobile. His face was marred by pitted chicken pox scars. He wore a black track suit with the word "Hickey" embroidered on the chest. A towel was draped around his neck. He had on black Nike sneakers. He regarded us disdainfully. "Was there anything else?"

Mr. Long glanced at Johnny and Marsha, then returned his attentions to me when I asked, "Is your brother here?"

"He's called Reverend Long."

"Okay. Is Reverend Long here?"

"Reverend Long is in conference just now."

"Can you interrupt him?"

"I can't. I'm sorry. He's preparing for the upcoming Heart of Our Saviour Celebration and has left strict instructions not to be disturbed."

"I see."

I stood silently, staring dead-eyed at Hickham Long.

"I guess that will that be all, then." Long glared at me dismissively, flashed a humorless grin, and turned away.

"Not exactly."

He turned back. "What not exactly?"

"Please inform Reverend Long that we're here on official business."

"Didn't you get the memo?" Long snapped, a regular pit bull. "He's not available."

"Then make him available."

"What are you, hard of hearing? It isn't going to happen, Officer."

"Sheriff," I said.

"Excuse me?"

"I'm the County Deputy Sheriff."

"Good for you, Mr. County Deputy Sheriff. It still isn't going to happen. Next time, call ahead for an appointment."

"Are you always such an obstructionist?"

This caught his attention.

"Obstructionist?"

"You know. Someone who manages to get in the way."

"I know the definition. Don't be condescending to me."

"I'm going to ask you one more time. Please inform Reverend Long that I'd like to speak with him."

A crooked smile broke out on Hickham Long's face. He waved his hand dismissively in my direction, turned his back, and started to walk away.

I grabbed him by the neck of his shirt and spun him around, clamped his arm, and twisted it up behind his back.

"Cuff him, Johnny," I said.

Johnny Kennerly jumped to Long's side, took the handcuffs from his kit belt, and cuffed Long's hands behind him. Long kicked out at him. Johnny stepped back.

Long snarled, flashing a row of yellowing teeth. "What in the fuck you think you're doing?"

"Book him," I told Johnny. "Read him his rights and put him in the cruiser."

I headed for the house.

"Hey," Hickham Long called out. "Where do you think you're going?"

I climbed the steps to the front porch.

Long wrested himself from Johnny's grasp and ran after me. When he reached the porch, he barreled into me, knocking me against the wall.

He raised his voice and called into the house, "Howard. Leonard. I need help."

He turned and faced me threateningly.

I called out to Johnny and Marsha. "Are you witnessing this?"

They both nodded their assent.

With his hands still bound behind him, Long rushed menacingly toward me. He lowered his head and attempted to butt me in the stomach.

I sidestepped him, whirled him around, and kicked him hard in the nuts. He went down as if he'd been shot.

"Pick him up and get him into the cruiser," I told Johnny, who helped the still-gasping Long to his feet. He hustled the moaning man to the cruiser, opened the rear door, and slammed him inside. He locked the vehicle's doors using his remote, making it impossible for Long to get out.

On the porch, I unholstered my Colt Combat Commander, press checked it, then clicked off the safety.

The front door swung open. Two men rushed out of the house wearing identical black suits and matching Oakley sunglasses. They were a whole lot tougher-looking than Jeffrey and much less friendly. They lurched to a halt in front of me, seeing my Colt pointed in their direction.

"Hands where I can see them," I said.

The men exchanged glances, then slowly raised their hands above their heads. I held my gun on the two men as Johnny Kennerly stepped up to each of them and in turn, frisked them. Both were carrying Beretta Bobcat semi-automatic pistols that he confiscated. I motioned for him to hand the weapons to Marsha Russo.

The front door opened again. I recognized the Reverend Barry Long, Junior, as he stepped outside. He quickly took the measure of what was going on.

"Gentlemen, gentlemen," he said. "What in heaven's name is happening here?"

He waved for his men to stand down, offered his hand, and introduced himself. "Barry Long."

I looked at him, then snapped on the safety and holstered my Colt. I shook the Reverend's hand.

"Buddy Steel. San Remo County Deputy Sheriff."

"Whatever did we do to warrant a visit from the Sheriff's office?"

"I'm here to see your wife."

"My wife?"

"Catharine. She is your wife, yes?"

"Of course she is. It's just that she's not in residence now."

Long turned to the two men. "I can handle this from here."

One of the men pointed to Marsha and whispered something in the Reverend's ear.

"I told you I'd handle it."

Reluctantly, with sideward glances at me, the two men filed back into the house. One of them stood just inside the ornate mahogany door frame, watching.

The Reverend Barry Long, Junior, had made his reputation as a humble preacher who claimed that his espousal of the issues of the common man had gained him access to God's ear. He referred to himself as The People's Pastor.

He was a ruggedly handsome man—blue-eyed, tall, and rock-star slim. He dressed in pressed work shirts and jeans, what he referred to as the people's clothing, except that unlike their garments, his bore the Armani label and were impeccably tailored. His snakeskin boots were polished to a high sheen. His trademark blue bandanna was tied loosely around his neck.

Eloquently and passionately he preached the values of family, worship, and common decency. On that platform, he built an ever-increasing worldwide following of loyalists who idolized him. He was an ecclesiastical phenomenon. His vast holdings bore testament to his stature.

Now he stood in front of me, beaming. "What is it you want to discuss with Catharine?"

"That's between her and me."

"I'm her husband. Is there something I should know about?"

"No."

"In other words, you're not going to tell me."

"Correct."

"And you believe I have no right to know."

"Correct again."

Long said nothing.

"Where might I find her?"

His eyes slid sideways. "She's gone to be with my sister back in LaGrange."

"She's in Tennessee?"

"Yes."

"Is there a contact number?"

"No."

"Excuse me?"

"She's not receiving calls just now," Long said.

"Perhaps she'll be willing to receive mine."

"Not likely."

"May I have her number just the same?"

Long stared stone-eyed at me for several moments. "Of course."

"And her address, as well."

"Certainly."

Long turned to the man standing behind the front door.

"Leonard, would you be so kind as to bring me Catharine's contact information?"

We stood awkwardly while Leonard went inside the house. After several moments he returned and handed a piece of paper to Reverend Long who, in turn, handed it to me. On it were written a series of telephone numbers and an address.

I looked at the paper, then handed it to Marsha. "Please call the top one."

Marsha took out her cell phone and punched in the number. "It's gone straight to voice mail."

"Leave a message. Ask her to phone me. Give her my cell number."

After Marsha had done so, I turned to Reverend Long.

"What are the other numbers?"

"My sister's cell phone. The number of the house at which they're staying."

"Will they all go unanswered?"

Long shrugged. "I would have no way of knowing."

After several moments, I said, "Thank you for your help."

I looked at Marsha and nodded to Johnny. We all started toward the cruiser.

The Reverend cleared his throat and took a step toward me. "I believe you have two of our weapons."

"We do," I responded.

"May I have them?"

"No."

"What?"

"No, you may not have them."

"They're licensed."

"I presumed as much."

"Then please return them."

"You can pick them up at the Sheriff's station."

"The station."

"Yes."

"Meaning you won't return them to us here."

"Correct."

"Why not?"

"Protocol."

"What protocol?"

"Sheriff's protocol."

Reverend Long glared at me.

I flashed him my most beatific smile. "Was there anything else?"

"My brother."

"What about him?"

"Surely you're not going to arrest him."

"I already have."

"On what charges?"

"Interfering with an officer in the performance of his duty. Assault. Obstruction of justice."

"He meant you no harm, Sheriff."

Long took a few more steps toward me. "The whereabouts of my house is public knowledge. People are constantly coming here trying to gain access to me and my family. My brother was only doing his job in trying to protect me."

"Protect you from the County Sheriff?"

A sheepish grin appeared on the Reverend's face. He didn't respond.

I stared at him for a while. He was brimming with confidence, certain he would prevail. I came to the realization that I didn't like him. But in the interests of comity, I decided to relent. I called out to Johnny. "Release the brother."

Johnny glanced at me, then walked to the cruiser and unlocked the doors. He assisted Hickham Long in exiting the vehicle. Once out, he removed Long's handcuffs.

Long took a few tentative steps away from the cruiser, still experiencing some pain. He winced visibly and stared weak-eyed at his brother.

"Thank you, Sheriff," the Reverend said. A heavenly smile made an appearance on his upturned face.

I smiled back, then got into the cruiser, followed by Marsha and Johnny. I lowered my window.

"It was sure nice meeting you boys," I said to the Long brothers.

Then I revved up the cruiser, drove down the winding driveway to the main gate, turned left and headed for the station.

Johnny swiveled to face me.

"What just happened back there?"

"The opening salvo."

"Meaning?"

"The Reverend Barry Long now knows we have an interest in the whereabouts of his wife. We've gotten his attention."

"Junior," Marsha said.

"Excuse me?"

"It's Junior. Barry Long, Junior. You wouldn't want to forget the Junior part."

"No, Marsha, I surely wouldn't. And thank you so much for that clarification."

"You're very welcome. I'd hate for you to get it wrong."

"I never knew you to be so considerate."

A wide grin appeared on her face. "Life is full of little surprises. So, what happens now?"

"We make every possible effort to contact Catharine Long, nee Catharine Morecombe."

"In LaGrange."

"Yes. We won't reach her, though. None of the numbers will answer."

"How do you know?"

"I'm the Sheriff's Deputy. I know everything."

Johnny snorted. "So why are we trying?"

"For the record. To keep it clean. I also want to undertake an investigation into the life of Catharine Long. I want to know everything about her. What she does. Where she goes. Where and how she came into contact with Barry Long."

I looked at Marsha.

"Junior," I added. "I also want to know about her family. Her parents. Her siblings. I want to know who her friends are, her interests, what she reads, what she thinks, the kind of panties she wears…everything."

"You're kidding about the panties, right?" Johnny said.

"The panties are a metaphor."

"What metaphor?"

"An illustration of the fact that there's nothing about Catharine Long that I don't want to know."

Johnny smiled at me. "You know what, Buddy?" he baited. "You're a seriously disturbed person."

"Thank you."

Chapter Five

The rain began in earnest. Raging winds whipped through the trees bringing down branches and foliage. In a few instances, they even toppled the trees themselves. Power lines were down. Drenching rains filled drainage outlets to overflowing. Those few souls who ventured out were soaked within minutes. The temperature dropped twenty degrees. It was the first monsoon-sized storm of the season and it was determined to break the previously held records for September. Our return to the office was slow going.

"So, how is he?" Johnny asked.

"Not so good," I said.

I had known Johnny Kennerly and Marsha Russo for years, both personally and professionally. Johnny had been deputized by my father at the start of his second term. He was a local boy, born and raised in Freedom, who had spent summers doing menial jobs around the station, fascinated by police work, absorbing all he could learn, and at the same time, ingratiating himself to my father.

He was smart, a quick study, and when he graduated from Roosevelt High in north Freedom, my father quietly used his influence to have him admitted to the state university in San Luis Obispo, California Polytechnic State University, Cal Poly as it was called, and paid the tuition out of his own pocket.

When Johnny graduated with honors, my father hired him and after two years with the department, elevated him to Undersheriff. He was like a second son to the old man, closer to him in many ways than I am.

"He won't talk about it. He shows up every day and goes to work," I said. "But he's having trouble talking and I can already feel him slipping away."

Marsha, seated in the back, nodded. "He is keeping his distance," she said. "At first I thought it was me, but I now I realize it's not."

I skirted around a fallen branch as we approached the outskirts of Freedom.

"How you doing?" Johnny asked.

I shrugged. "Conflicted. I know I agreed to do this. I don't suppose I had much choice. But sometimes at night, when I'm lying there staring into the dark, I don't feel so good about it. I left a life I was building for myself, and now I'm here, at his beck and call again. So far he's been good, but one of these days he's sure as shit gonna unload on me and I'm going to regret my choice. Regardless of his illness. It took every ounce of nerve I had to get out from under him. And as the song goes, 'Look At Me Now.'"

"You never know, Buddy," Marsha said. "Illness does strange things to people."

"Are you referring to him or to me?"

"Both of you."

• • ● • •

I was staring out my office window, watching the last of the storm when Johnny came in and sat in the chair across from me.

"You were right," he said.

"About?"

"None of the numbers answer. They just ring and ring."

"I knew it."

"I contacted the LaGrange phone company. Apart from Catharine's cell phone, none of the other numbers are functional. They were once registered to Barry Long, but they haven't been in service for at least two years."

"What about birth records?"

"State records list the birth of a Mary Catharine Morecombe on July 2, 1994, in Memphis."

"Is Mary Catharine Morecombe an only child?"

"You mean has she any siblings?"

"Yes."

"None. In fact, Mary Louise Morecombe, nee Carter, Catharine's mother, died in childbirth."

"Survivors?"

"Only the father, Albert Morecombe."

"Still alive?"

"In an assisted living facility in Jackson. Suffering from advanced dementia."

"He never remarried?"

"Not according to the records."

"And you're sure there are no other children?"

"Yes."

"Let me get this straight. The LaGrange phone company is saying that there are no Longs listed there?"

"They are. None currently. At least none that can be traced to Barry Long."

"What's Long's sister's name again?"

"Margaret."

"And there are no listings for a Margaret Long?"

"Correct."

"Well, hello, Reverend Barry."

"He lied to us, Buddy. Why would he do that?"

"Beats me."

"What are you going to do?"

"When does this Heart of Our Saviour mishigas begin?"

"Mishigas?" Johnny said.

"A euphemism."

"For?"

"Insanity. When does it start?"

"A week from Friday."

"So we have a little time."

"Time for what?"

"For a time when the good Reverend will be otherwise engaged."

"Meaning?"

"It's a major event, yes?"

"It is if you consider a thousand or more Evangelicals packed into Long Pavilion an event."

"And it lasts for three days."

"Yes."

"So it's likely the Reverend and his security boys will all be in residence at the Pavilion."

"It's likely they're already there. Remember those

vans we saw at the mansion? They were packed and ready to go."

"Don't I remember something about the entire Long family appearing at these annual Holy Moly affairs?"

"That sounds right," Johnny said.

"But for this one, Mrs. Holy Moly is allegedly out of town and unavailable."

Johnny nodded.

"What's wrong with this picture? Johnny, would you please ask Marsha to phone Judge Feinstein and ask him to issue a warrant for the Long house?"

"What reason does she give?"

"She swears him to secrecy and tells him suspicion of murder."

"You think he murdered her?"

"I don't know, Johnny. First, a frightened nanny suggests she may have been killed. Then the Long brothers run us around in circles. Next week is their annual boogie boogie hooyah event and, for all intents and purposes, her holiness, the prominent wife, seems to have gone missing. I think while the mice are away is the perfect time to have a closer look at their nest. Maybe there's a clue or two lurking about."

"So you're going to serve the warrant when he's not there?"

"I am."

"He's not gonna like that."

"You think?"

Chapter Six

I decided to take the long way home. Give myself some space to muse while perusing the homeland, so to speak. I headed for the northwestern corner of the county and meandered through its namesake capital, El Ciudad de San Remo, a small picturesque village noted for its Spanish Colonial-style architecture, plus El Calle de San Remo, a miracle mile of modern skyscrapers and trendy shops.

It had turned into a storybook California day, the golden sun high in a cloudless sky, temperatures in the low seventies. I turned onto Highway 101 and zigzagged my way south, passing through vast stretches of undeveloped coastline, the roiling sea and an occasional flurry of homes to the west, the verdant Sierra Madre mountains to the east.

San Remo, like Santa Barbara, its sister county to the south, had been discovered and developed centuries ago by Spanish explorers. Long content to bask in the shadow of its more popular southern neighbor, sleepy San Remo County slowly began to wake up at the turn of the twentieth century when the movie industry arrived and construction began on the 101, the Pacific Coast Highway.

From 1910 to 1922, Santa Barbara was the unlikely epicenter of California silent film production, attracting to its shores stars such as Douglas Fairbanks, Lon Chaney, Jr., Lilian Gish, and the ubiquitous Charlie Chaplin.

Beguiled by its inherent beauty, industry denizens began gobbling up acres of spectacular mountainous terrain, and in short order spacious mansions and haciendas dotted the hills overlooking the Santa Barbara Channel and the Pacific.

Sensing a need for a quieter, more upscale version of Santa Barbara to be situated in San Remo County, the canny developer, Reinhold Lamy, founded the township of Freedom in the late 1920s.

While Santa Barbara suffered earthquakes, floods, massive fires, even an aborted attack by a Japanese submarine near the end of World War II, Freedom, under Lamy's tightly held reins, quietly grew and prospered.

Numbers of the film notables who had initially settled in Santa Barbara, now saw the potential for a more exclusive and secluded living experience in the lushly forested, hidden hills of Freedom. Although many had relocated to the newly established communities of Hollywood and Beverly Hills, where the talkies were flourishing, the prospect of being part of an elite coastal community comprised mainly of resplendent second homes, a mere two-hour drive from L.A., proved irresistible to myriad A-listers.

Freedom became a haven of exclusivity, elegance and beauteous isolation, a private wonderland not only for filmdom's rich and powerful, but for the wealthy industrialists of Northern California as well.

Under the auspices of a succession of omnipotent county executives, plus the continued presence of an army of highly up-skilled security personnel, Freedom turned into one of Southern California's most select destinations.

But it was my father's encroaching incapacity, not its natural beauty, that caused my hat to once again hang there. Although it was my childhood home, it had been for me a kind of psychological prison from which I believed I had escaped, only to discover that my escape was illusory and that I was once again wedded to a fate I had long ago eschewed.

I wished it wasn't so.

But wishing gets you nowhere.

Chapter Seven

Wilma Hansen, the dispatcher, buzzed me. "Mayor Goodnow on Line Two."

"Tell her I'm out of the country."

"Tell her yourself. Line Two."

I picked up the call. "Your Honor."

"Don't *Your Honor* me, Buddy," Regina said. "What are you up to?

"Excuse me?"

"What have you got going with Barry Long?"

"Junior," I said.

"What?"

"Junior. Barry Long, Junior."

"Don't mess with me, Buddy. What's going on?"

"Mrs. Junior has gone missing."

"Missing?"

"Yes. She allegedly vanished a week or so ago. She's nowhere to be found. Reverend Barry told me she was in LaGrange. With his sister. But we've been unable to locate either of them there."

"Surely there's an explanation for that. This is no time to be hassling the Longs, Buddy. They're knee-deep into their Heart of Our Saviour preparations and, in case you've forgotten, it's a very big boon for business here."

Mayor Goodnow was halfway through her second term and was widely acknowledged as a great friend to the Freedom business community.

Previously she had been the Deputy Mayor, a longtime associate of her predecessor, who had been forced to step down due to term limits. She picked up his baton, adopted his agenda, and was generally docile except when she faced perceived challenges to her policies.

She met my father at the county courthouse, where both the Mayor's and the Sheriff's offices were housed. They noticed each other almost immediately. Both had lost spouses to illness. Both were lonely. Their proximity sparked a romance.

They quickly married in a small civil ceremony, attended by Regina's twin sons and by my sister and me. She moved into my father's house and proceeded to redecorate it from top to bottom, removing any trace of my mother in the process.

We enjoyed an uneasy truce, Regina and I. I was the only one of the children who lived in Freedom and the three of us pussy-footed around each other, avoiding conflict as best we could.

"What exactly is it you're saying, Regina?"

"Don't escalate this thing, Buddy."

"Don't escalate the investigation into Mrs. Long's disappearance?"

"Yes."

"No."

"What?"

"No. It's escalating."

"Damn it, Buddy. Can't it wait?"

"A prominent resident of Freedom has disappeared, leaving behind a distraught child and a husband who's withholding information regarding her whereabouts. I'm going to investigate this, Regina. Surely, you wouldn't want it any other way."

She didn't say anything.

"I didn't think so. I'll let you know what I find out."

After a brief silence, Regina said, "Will we be seeing you for dinner this evening?"

"I wouldn't miss it for the world."

"Try not to exaggerate, Buddy. Seven o'clock."

"I'll be there."

I ended the call.

Marsha Russo appeared in my doorway. "Obviously, the Reverend holds some sway with Her Honor."

"Obviously."

"So?"

"What's the status of the warrant?"

"The paperwork has been faxed to Judge Feinstein. I'm waiting for him to sign and return it."

The intercom buzzed. I picked it up.

"Looks like you hit the Perfecta," Wilma said.

"What's that supposed to mean?"

"ADA Alfred Wilder awaits the pleasure of a word with you."

"Jesus."

"Should I tell him you're incommunicado?"

"No. I'll take it."

I picked up the phone. "Skip," I said,"what a lovely surprise."

"Don't *lovely surprise* me, Buddy. If there's a piece of shit anywhere in Freedom, you'll be the first to step in it."

"Do you think you could clarify that statement?"

"Barry Long," Wilder said.

"Junior."

"What?"

"Junior. Barry Long, Junior."

"Dammit, Buddy. The law firm of Kornbluth and Kurtz has fallen on us like a thousand-pound weight."

I chose not to say anything, aware of the fact that my silence would further aggravate him.

"Murray Kornbluth himself, Buddy. Murray Fucking Kornbluth. Exactly what we needed."

"I hope he wasn't hurt in the fall."

"Don't crap around. What in the hell is going on?"

"Mrs. Barry Long, Junior, has vanished."

"Kornbluth denies that."

"Why don't you try to find her then, Skip? See if you have better luck than I've had."

"Listen to me, Buddy. Kornbluth says that Mrs. Long suffered a bit of a breakdown and is currently on a sabbatical from her duties with the Foundation."

"Did he offer to prove that assertion?"

"He's Murray Kornbluth, for crissakes. He doesn't have to prove anything."

"And if he's wrong?"

"Lytell wants you to lay off of this."

"Lytell does?"

"Yes."

"Michael Lytell and Murray Kornbluth. Jesus. Two peas in the same overprivileged cesspod."

"Did you hear anything I've been saying, Buddy?"

"Listen, Skip, yesterday I had a visit from the Long family nanny. She's who told me about Mrs. Long's disappearance and about how she was instructed by Reverend Barry to take charge of the care and feeding of the boy in his mother's absence. Apparently the kid has become despondent. She also mentioned in passing how frightened she was of Long's security personnel and how she believed they might well have offed the Missus. She told me this on her way out of town and into hiding. When I went to investigate this assertion, I got stonewalled. First by the Reverend's malevolent brother, then by the Reverend himself."

"So?"

"My suspicions have been raised. I don't like what I saw at the mansion. I don't like that the Reverend lied to me. I don't like any of it."

"What are you going to do?"

"I'm going to carry on an investigation until I'm satisfied with the results."

"So Reverend Long is guilty until proven innocent. Is that how it goes, Buddy?"

"It is, if that's how you choose to read it. In point of fact, and with all due respect, I don't really give a rat's ass what either you or Michael Lytell think. I've got reasonable cause to investigate the alleged disappearance of Mary Catharine Long, and I intend to do so."

"And if we seek to enjoin?"

"You have no grounds. And if you insist on harassing me, I'll invite the national media to the party and embarrass the Reverend, Murray Kornbluth, and our esteemed District Attorney. You, too, Skip."

"Is that what you want me to tell the District Attorney?"

"Tell him whatever you want. I'll inform you of my findings. I'll try to get it done on a timely basis. Assuming Reverend Long doesn't further complicate matters."

"You better pray you come up with something, Buddy."

"Would I were a praying man."

"Maybe now would a good time to become one."

Chapter Eight

Marsha Russo turned her attention to the main entrance where Sheriff's Deputy P.J. Lincoln had arrived, accompanied by Sarah Kaplow, the town librarian, whom I'd known since I was a boy. They entered the office, both dressed for rain.

Sarah Kaplow was a firebrand, short, stout, and plainly dressed. She was without makeup, or fashionable hairstyle, or any type of pretension. She was sixty if she was a day, possessed of a lively intelligence and a warm and charismatic personality. She was a town fixture and much beloved.

"Sarah." I welcomed her to my office. "And on such a wet day."

"Good morning, Buddy. You have to know my visit is important, otherwise I'd still be planted at my desk, dry as toast."

"What brings you, Sarah?"

Deputy Lincoln answered. "Sarah has some knowledge of Catharine Long, who turns out to be a member of the Library Foundation Board. She told me a few things I thought you might find interesting."

"Okay."

"I've come to know and quite like Catharine Long," Sarah said. "She's deceptively intelligent and a great supporter of the library."

"Why deceptively?"

"She's smarter than one would expect from a girl born in the Tennessee lowlands and she's not afraid to show it."

"Okay."

"Lately, though, she's been pretty stressed."

"How so?"

"I feel somewhat uncomfortable revealing information that was told to me in confidence."

"Don't be. Catharine Long has disappeared and I'm trying to find her."

Sarah briefly wrestled with this conundrum, silently clenching and unclenching her fists. "I understand. All right. Catharine has had some serious disagreements with her husband. About her role in his ministry. About their son. About their relationship. She's very angry with him.

"Does the expression chauvinist pig ring a bell with you, Buddy? She says he doesn't give her any credit for the role she's played in his success. Now he's trying to push her into a backseat. He wants to elevate his son to celebrity status. At age five, no less. According to Catharine, the Reverend is planning to introduce little Barry to his congregation on the first night of this year's Celebration. They call him Three, by the way. He's being trained to sing a revisionist interpretation of "Nearer My God to Thee" that's scheduled to open the ceremonies. Which Catharine greatly opposes. She doesn't want any son of hers turning into a dancing bear, if you get my drift. This has caused a great deal of stress between the Longs."

"What did Catharine do about that?"

"I'm not altogether certain. She did phone me, but during the call, someone interrupted her and it was terminated. I've not heard from her since."

"What did she say?"

"Not a lot, I'm afraid. She was clearly upset and had just begun to get into it when the call ended. I tried to phone her back but was told she was unavailable."

"After which she disappeared."

"So it would appear."

After a few moments, Sarah said, "There's something else."

"Okay."

"Although she didn't go into detail, she recently hinted they had money problems."

"I thought they were raking it in hand-over-fist."

"That may be a misconception. She's a good girl, Buddy. And she's very much alone. I hope she's all right."

"Thank you for this, Sarah. I'll let you know as soon as I learn something."

Sarah wrestled herself to her feet. "I'd appreciate that."

Chapter Nine

We were sitting in the breakfast nook, sipping gin and tonics, watching the dusky twilight turn dark through walls of paned glass.

"This was your mother's favorite room," my father reminisced.

I nodded in acknowledgement.

He asked me to come early. For drinks and what he referred to as some frank talk. The old pair of khaki slacks and the washed-out blue sweatshirt were indicative of his diminution of spirit, a low-grade depression that surrounded him like cloud cover.

"This isn't how I had envisioned things. This was going to be the term in which I cemented my legacy. By the time it's over, I'll be lucky if I can even move my lips."

"Is that really true? Aren't there drugs that slow the progress?"

"There's no cure, Buddy. It's progressive and fatal. And no fun in the process."

He leaned forward and stared at me through rueful eyes. His voice displayed only a measure of its once formidable power.

"I'm counting on you."

"I'll do everything I can."

"Do you actually mean that or are you just flapping your gums?"

"Excuse me?"

"I can't go through this to the finish, Buddy. I'm not going to play the end game. There'll come a tipping point. And when that arrives, the ride ends for me. That's when I'll need you."

"I'm not sure I like the sound of this."

"I'll do the research and the planning. But when the time comes, I'm going to need you to help me turn out the lights."

"Whoa. Hold on. You're talking assisted suicide here."

"I am."

"That's a big deal, Dad. I need to think about it. Why me and not Regina?"

"What's in front of me is irrevocable. One way or the other. I refuse to go out a vegetable. When the time comes, Regina will be useless. It's you I need, Buddy. There's nothing to think about."

We were interrupted by Her Honor, who entered the room like a windstorm, switching on all of the lights in her wake.

"What are you boys doing sitting here in the dark?" She bent over my father and kissed his forehead. "It's glum in here."

She flashed me her look.

"Good evening, Buddy," she said. "Word is you had a stressful day."

She turned to my father. "Buddy had a go-around

with the Assistant District Attorney. Not to mention assorted members of the Long family."

When my father didn't say anything, she went on. "Are you sure this is what you want the Sheriff's Department to be doing, Burton?"

My father eyed her warily. "What is it you're saying, Regina?"

"Only what I've already told Buddy. Maybe this isn't the opportune moment to be turning up the heat under the Longs."

"If I'm not mistaken," my father said, "Mrs. Long has gone missing?"

"Not according to Murray Kornbluth."

"Who won't produce her so as to put an end to the speculation."

My stepmother poured a splash of gin over a handful of ice cubes. She downed a large swallow, poured herself another and sat. "According to the family, she's had a breakdown."

"So?"

"She's resting."

"Where?"

"They didn't say."

"They need to produce her," my father said. "Or at the very least, if she's been institutionalized, they need to reveal where she is so we can check her out for ourselves."

"So you're supporting Buddy in this?"

"That's not what it's about, Regina, and you know it. A Long family servant has suggested foul play. The Reverend, in turn, misled us. Mrs. Long is nowhere to be found. It's time for them to shit or get off the pot."

"God, Burton. Must you always be so crude?"

He snorted.

Regina turned to me. "Allow me to offer you a bit of mayoral advice, Buddy. You're making a huge mistake. You don't stand a snowball's chance in hell against the Longs. All you'll succeed in doing is embarrassing yourself and your office."

My father struggled to his feet. "That's enough, Regina. In the future, please keep your nose out of our business. I'm sure you have enough to do just trying to govern the city."

He gazed at his watch, and pointed toward the dining room. "Dinnertime."

Regina stood and, with a scowl, exited.

I turned to my father, who was staring bullets at me. "Don't forget, Buddy. One hand washes the other."

Chapter Ten

I poured myself a straight gin and thought about the evening just passed.

My father had vanished into his mortality. He was distracted and fearful. He had always been a physical presence, active and energized, an imposing figure, tall and classically handsome. He frowned on weakness and disability. He was the Sheriff. He perceived himself the equivalent of the noble Sheriffs of yore, powerful and omnipotent. Now he was dying.

Regina, despite being limited by the narrowness of her thought, had been elected Mayor to serve the economic interests of a small town. She was unwavering in her quest to succeed. At the outset, she was good-hearted and kind, but over time, she had developed a veneer of toughness that she wrapped around herself like a Snuggie.

The dynamic between her and my father had come crashing down, leaving each of them in search of a toehold on a new reality that would carry them into their uncertain future. I had re-entered their universe at exactly that moment.

After seasons of living apart, I was now the guardian of my father's escutcheon and the protector of his diminishing powers. An unwitting participant in his "one hand washes the other" philosophy.

I finished the gin and poured another.

Then I inserted the disc into the DVD player and settled in to watch it. It was taken during last year's Heart of Our Saviour Celebration.

The Long family was on full display. Reverend Barry was seen welcoming the faithful. Catharine stood beside him, smiling. Four-year-old Three stood between them.

The response was deafening. The camera panned the crowd and frequently settled on the enthralled expressions that lit up the faces of those in attendance.

I hit the fast-forward button. After several moments, when I saw only Catharine on the screen, I pressed *Play*.

She was twenty-two at the time, fresh-looking, pretty, delivering some kind of homespun homily regarding family and worship. A close-up revealed heavily applied makeup covering an acne outbreak on her chin.

Her thick fair hair was cut short and was stylishly chaotic. She had on a colorful print dress that seemed better suited to a high school social than a revivalist Celebration. She was full-bodied and by the way she moved, proud of it.

She had an appealingly girlish charm. Hers was a pleasant voice and she spoke well. Her smile brightened the screen. I found her attractive and, for her age, quite self-possessed.

She obviously made a powerful impression on the crowd.

Her speech was covered by at least nine cameras, all placed at various positions around the arena, allowing for different angles and sizes of coverage. Her performance appeared well-rehearsed and carefully edited.

The camera director provided us with wide shots as she strolled among the assembled, including coverage of adoring fans fawning over her as she passed.

When her message was more intimate, we were shown medium close-ups, many including wide-eyed admirers.

When her performance was at its most commanding, we saw her in extreme close-up. Full screen. Her eyes ablaze, her mouth pouty and tantalizing, her concentration compellingly intense. The effect of the camera coverage, wide and tight, mobile and stationary, was mesmerizing. Movie star mesmerizing.

When she finished, they gave her a standing ovation and as she walked through the audience one last time, a hush fell as the faithful parted respectfully and lovingly so she could stroll among them unimpeded.

All of it captured on video and for sale in the lobby.

I watched for a while longer, then fast-forwarded again, stopping when Reverend Barry appeared. He was all energy, kinetic and smooth. His voice was seductive and compelling. He was in constant motion, moving easily among the crowd, stopping to touch a hand here, make deep eye contact there. His followers clearly adored him, which the myriad TV cameras dutifully captured.

But cameras don't lie. There was something disingenuous about him. His performance felt manipulative and his piety seemed forced. To me, his goodness and light were insincere and snarky, at odds with a dark energy that hovered menacingly beneath the surface of his personality.

He wouldn't take kindly to criticism or contradiction. I could see how retribution might be a factor in his professional and personal conduct. He looked like a "my way or the highway" kind of guy. Lord help the person who got in his way.

Although he had the crowd in the palm of his hand, I found him anything but ingratiating. Barry Long, Junior, seemed a dangerous man.

I ejected the DVD and turned off the TV. I poured myself another gin and thought about the Longs.

Catharine was a star attraction and the camera magnified her charisma. Perhaps she presented a threat to the Reverend, a challenge to his popularity and his authority. He wouldn't share celebrity easily. Especially not with his beautiful, dewy-eyed young wife. In Barry Long's universe, everyone had a place. Overstepping boundaries could bring about repercussions.

My curiosity was piqued. "Why did he lie? What happened to her? Where is she? Might he really have killed her?"

The gin had made its point. More than just slightly loaded, I turned off the lights and went to bed.

Chapter Eleven

The morning brought with it heavy clouds accompanied by a misting rain. When I gazed out the window of my rented condo that overlooked the bay, I could barely see anything. I straightened up, put on my raingear, and headed out.

I pulled my Sheriff's cruiser to a stop in front of Saint Theresa's, one of Freedom's two Cathedrals, this one located in the north end, close to the sea.

Built in the 1890s in the Gothic-revival style, the concrete structure had withstood earthquakes, monsoons, and more than its share of ocean-precipitated deterioration.

The 1,100-seat sanctuary boasted a dozen stained-glass windows, each depicting an incident in the life of Lord Jesus. I zipped up my waterproof parka, lowered my Sheriff's cap, and headed for the rectory.

Father Francis Dugan, a local institution and the acknowledged leader of the Freedom religious community, greeted me warmly.

Father Dugan's age was a mystery. He had been in place for as long as anyone could remember. He came toward me, slower of step than I remembered, but with the same fierce determination for which he was noted.

An infectious grin brightened his wizened face. His eyes were agleam with wisdom and mischief. His warmth of spirit was contagious. A spiritual being, he was a friend to all, regardless of race, creed, or color.

He led me into his office and offered me a seat in one of the two worn armchairs in a corner of the room, below a dormer window that overlooked the small vegetable garden that Father Dugan lovingly tended. I declined his offer of a beverage.

"What brings you to Saint Theresa's, Buddy? Not that you ever need a reason. You're always a welcome sight."

"Thank you, Father."

Father Dugan sat back in his chair and rested his legs on a small hassock. He sighed contentedly when he finally settled upon the right comfort level.

"Information," I said.

"Excuse me?"

"It's fairly common knowledge that when it comes to matters of the spiritual community, you're the Oracle."

"Ha! That's a good one. The Oracle. I like that."

"It's true."

"Let's say I keep my ears open and, on occasion, I hear something worthwhile. But only on the very rare occasion."

"Rubbing the blarney stone this morning, are we, Father?"

"Could it be that you're on to me, Buddy?"

"Only if being on to you is an acknowledgement that you're the foremost purveyor of the most closely guarded secrets in Freedom."

"You give me too much credit."

"Fess up, Francis."

"What's the subject?"

"Barry Long, Junior."

Father Francis shifted his position and looked more closely at me. "Playing with fire, are we, Buddy?"

"I've hit a wall."

"Meaning?"

"I'm not certain I can answer that question."

"If the conditions were right, I might be able to help you," the Father hinted.

"What conditions?"

"We never had this discussion."

"What discussion?"

Father Francis smiled. "Reverend Long's name has been on people's lips of late."

"How so?"

"Service providers to religious organizations often rely heavily on trust, particularly when it comes to issues of credit."

"Would it be out of line to suggest that instead of parable, you spoke English?"

Father Francis wagged his finger at me. "Don't be impudent, Buddy."

"Who, me?"

He chuckled. "It seems that a few of Barry Long's suppliers are experiencing a disruption in the flow of money owed them for services rendered."

"You mean they're not being paid on a timely basis?"

"I'm hearing that some aren't being paid at all."

"How could that be?"

"Good question."

"And the answer?"

"Look to the father."

"Excuse me?"

"Barry Long, Senior. All roads lead to him."

"Let me get this straight. Suppliers to the Heart of Our Saviour Ministry aren't being paid?"

"In a number of instances."

"Why not? Isn't the Long Ministry drowning in capital?"

"You'd think."

"Are you suggesting that the Longs are having financial difficulties?"

Father Francis shrugged.

"And that the root of these difficulties lies with Barry Long, Senior?"

The Father pushed the hassock away and struggled to his feet.

"That's all I know, Buddy. You'll have to make do with it."

I stood. "Thank you, Father."

"I'm going to say something I'll deny ever having said."

I nodded.

"In the spiritual community, there's an unflattering epithet that's generally applied to the Long family. They're frequently referred to as, 'The son, his brother, and the unholy dickhead.'" Father Dugan followed this by making the sign of the cross in the air. "If you get my drift," he added, a mischievous smile brightening his face.

Chapter Twelve

My cell phone started buzzing. When I picked up the call, Marsha Russo said, "Judge Feinstein demurred."

"He demurred?"

"I just said that."

"Why?"

"According to his clerk, the judge wanted no part of this furball."

"Somebody got to him."

"Maybe. Now what?"

"We find a jurist whose opinions aren't subject to outside influence."

"You have someone in mind?"

"I might."

"Where are you?"

"About to make a surprise visit to Long Pavilion."

"What for?"

"A look-see."

"Good luck with that."

"Thanks. I'll call you."

I pulled the Wrangler to a stop in front of the Pavilion, a block-and-mortar structure that had been constructed in the late 1960s as a theatre-in-the-round. Music Circus Enterprises, a San Diego-based real estate company, developed the Pavilion and widened its business interests by creating a West Coast chain of arena-style venues in which they presented stage shows and live concerts, all of them featuring big-name entertainers.

Their idea was to bring star performers into suburban bedroom communities and create a newly imagined revenue stream. Movie stars appeared in roadshow editions of musicals and comedies. Mickey Rooney, Carol Channing, and Lana Turner once played the Pavilion, as did Jerry Lewis, Harry Belafonte, and most notably, Frank Sinatra.

The concept was a great success and thrived until sometime after the millennium, when the mega-show phenomenon gathered steam, filling sports arenas and stadiums that offered larger seating capacities. Music Circus Enterprises called it quits in 2004.

The site sat empty for several years until it was purchased in 2012 by the Long family, who poured considerable sums into a series of major renovations. It was a sizable property, with parking for hundreds of cars and seating for more than a thousand.

The building was situated in the center of a circular parking lot. It put me in mind of the Great Western Forum in Los Angeles, where the Lakers once played and where Jack Nicholson paraded his unabashed fanaticism in front of worldwide TV cameras.

The round stage remained where it had originally been constructed, in the bottom center of the arena, surrounded by ever-widening rows of seats that climbed dramatically heavenward toward the building's main floor, which was at ground level.

The Longs re-invigorated the space by replacing the narrow seats with more ergonomically appropriate ones. They brightened its industrial look with untold gallons of more colorful paint and enhanced it further by installing a collection of backlit light-boxes, each placed at the top of an aisle, each offering a highly stylized, stained-glass etching of a notable Biblical event.

The dressing room area had been totally reconceived. The star suite was converted into living quarters for the Long family, fashioned after the elegantly appointed luxury apartment that had been created for Celine Dion at Caesar's Palace in Las Vegas.

Smaller quarters were carved out for use either as office space or accommodations for other members of the family's entourage, and luminaries and visitors entertained by the Longs.

I made my way inside the Pavilion's main entrance. The lobby featured a fifteen-window box-office; a gift shop brimming with Heart of Our Saviour products, including clothing, home furnishings, and souvenir geegaws; and three fast-food and beverage concessions.

Where photos of Jerry Seinfeld and Robin Williams once hung, were dozens of larger-than-life-sized renderings of Barry Long, Junior, captured in various poses of rapturous ecstasy, all of them for sale.

I hurried across the lobby and stepped through a pair of gilt-edged double doors into the arena itself, where I spotted numbers of workmen engaged in a variety of activities.

Scaffolding had been constructed on the stage and a pair of young men were attaching theatre-style lighting instruments onto a metal grid that would later be raised to the ceiling above. Beneath the stage was an orchestra pit where a man in a white uniform was tuning a Steinway grand piano.

I had just begun to circle the arena in search of the living quarters when I spotted a young woman wearing a plain black shift over a white button-down blouse hurrying toward me.

"Welcome to Long Pavilion," she said breathlessly as she approached. "My name is Rosemary. I'm sorry to have to tell you this, but the arena is closed. You need to step outside."

"I was just looking around."

"I understand, but I'm afraid you have to step outside just the same."

She appeared to be in her mid- to late-twenties, plain-looking and self-conscious, devoid of makeup or any visible sense of personal style, but zealously earnest.

"Please." She pointed to the nearest door and urged me to accompany her there. "I'm sorry, but because of the upcoming Heart of Our Saviour Celebration, the tours have been temporarily suspended."

She edged me in the direction of the lobby.

"So I can't look around?"

"I'm sorry."

"Even just a little?"

"Again, I'm sorry."

"Because of the Celebration?"

"Yes."

"Can I at least purchase a picture or two of Reverend Long? My mother is such a fan."

"I'm sorry. Nothing's open."

"She'll be so disappointed."

"I'm sorry."

"Is there any way I can convince you to stop saying that?"

"Saying what?"

"I'm sorry. It sounds so insincere."

She clearly didn't know what to say next.

"Does the Reverend live here?" I asked.

"Here in the Pavilion?"

"Yes."

"I'm sorry, but I'm not at liberty to give out that information."

"There you go again."

"I think you should leave."

"Me?"

"Yes. You."

"But I've hardly seen anything."

"I'm sorry."

Chapter Thirteen

I drove slowly around the exterior of the Pavilion. In back, I noticed the stage door and beyond it, another separate entrance brandishing a sign that read, *Private. No Admittance.* Several cars were parked in assigned spaces. I pulled into a spot marked *Visitor Parking* and headed for the *No Admittance* entrance. I pulled the handle and, to my surprise, the door opened.

I stepped into a giant foyer, a large space containing any number of chairs and benches, lamps and tables, and walls adorned with billboard-size framed photos of the Reverend Barry looking toward the heavens, his arms outstretched, a rapturous smile adorning his face.

There were two other doors in the foyer. I tried the closest one, but it was locked. The second, however, wasn't. I opened it and stepped into what appeared to be family quarters. I walked tentatively through a handsomely appointed living area and into an adjoining playroom, with teddy-bear wallpaper and undersized furniture. Toys and picture books were scattered everywhere.

A young man in a black suit walked swiftly in my direction.

"I'm sorry," he said, "this area is off limits. You'll have to leave."

He took hold of my arm and attempted to hustle me outside. In response, I grabbed his wrist and twisted it backward, forcing him off balance and sending him plummeting to the floor.

"No touchee," I said.

"Robert," the man cried out.

Within seconds, two other men, also in black suits, came rushing into the playroom. These men were little more than thugs in suits. I understood why Rosalita Gonzalez feared them. Spotting me, one of them began yelling. "Who the fuck are you?"

"I was hoping to see Reverend Long."

"You're off limits."

"The door was open."

"It should have been locked."

"But it wasn't. Now that I'm here, couldn't I have a moment with the Reverend?"

"No."

"Why not?"

"Listen to me, pal. There are two ways you can leave. Either of your own accord. Or on a gurney. Your choice."

"A gurney?"

"You heard me."

He stepped closer to me.

"Okay, okay." I raised my hands as if in surrender.

I turned and headed for the door. The man walked beside me. Once outside, he shoved me away. "Don't come back. You're no longer welcome here."

"Not even for the Heart of Our Saviour Celebration?"

"You heard me."

"That's not a very spiritual attitude."

"That your Jeep?"

"It is."

"I'd advise you plant your ass inside it and then get the fuck out of here."

The man took a step toward me.

I flashed him my most sincere smile, then climbed into the Wrangler and drove off.

Chapter Fourteen

At the Hall of Justice reception desk, I asked the attendant for the whereabouts of Judge Ezekiel Azenberg's chambers. After checking my credentials, she provided me with the information.

I climbed three flights of stairs and located Room 305. There was no identifying sign on the door. Hesitant to enter unannounced, I knocked twice. After several moments, Judge Azenberg appeared in the doorway.

"Yes," he said.

"Judge Azenberg," I said. "I'm Deputy Sheriff Buddy Steel."

"Do I know you?"

"You probably know my father."

"Burton Steel?"

"Yes."

"Come in. Come in."

Judge Azenberg stepped aside so I could enter. Once we were seated, the judge said, "What brings you to my chambers, Mr. Steel?"

"Buddy."

"Buddy, it is."

"Forgive me for showing up unannounced, but something's come up that might be worthy of your attention."

Judge Azenberg looked at me questioningly. He wasn't a young man, but he had about him an air of youth. He wore a gray V-necked cashmere sweater over neatly pressed blue slacks. He had a full head of white hair. Smile lines adorned the corners of his mouth.

"It's about the Reverend Barry Long, Junior," I said.

"What about him?"

I explained the circumstances that prompted my visit.

"And you want me to issue the warrant?"

"I do."

Judge Azenberg sat silently for a while. "How certain are you about this?"

"Certain enough to believe that something untoward is going on in his universe."

"And you believe he may have killed her?"

"I'm not willing to go that far. I have no proof she's dead. But she's missing and my efforts to find her are being thwarted by the Reverend and his associates. I don't appreciate it and I very much want to take it to the next level."

"Which would be a search of their premises."

"Yes."

"What is it you expect to find?"

"I'm not exactly certain. I don't expect to discover any foul play, but there might well be a clue or two lying around that could point me in the right direction."

"The right direction being?"

"The one leading to Catharine Long."

Judge Azenberg sat in quiet contemplation for several more moments. "All right. Send me the paperwork. I'll sign it."

"Thank you, Your Honor."

"No need for thanks. I'm persuaded by your argument and, equally as important, by your concern for the welfare of Mrs. Long. As we used to say in law school, '*agis quo adis.*'"

"Which means?"

"Do what you have to do."

Chapter Fifteen

The directory in the lobby listed the Rosin & Rosin Advertising Agency as occupying offices on the top floor of the four-story office building located in downtown Freedom.

I stepped off the elevator and pushed through the glass doors that led to the agency's outer office. An unmanned receptionist's desk stood guard over the entrance to the inner sanctum.

The walls of the small waiting room were formed of smoked-glass panels that were backlit from inside. An industrial gray three-seater sofa was positioned in front of one of the panels, along with a side table, a square-based modern lamp, and a wooden rack that held a number of haphazardly arranged magazines.

I stood in the empty room for several moments, then walked past the receptionist's desk and through one of the smoked-glass doors. Inside was a narrow hallway separating a handful of cubicles, each of them doorless, featuring glass-paneled walls. I peered into each cubicle searching for signs of life. The occupant of one of them looked up when I appeared.

He was forty something, bearded and shaggy haired, dressed in jeans and a long-sleeved Polo shirt over which he wore a red fleece vest. "Did you bring the check?"

I didn't respond.

"Did Ms. Lebersfeld give you the check?"

I shrugged.

"You're from Lebersfeld and Klein?"

"No."

"You're not here with the check."

"Correct."

Now the man didn't say anything.

An attractive young woman materialized from one of the nearby cubicles, wearing a pale gray hoodie over black tights, carrying with her several pages of advertisement mockups. She shifted the pages in order to hold them more easily. "Who exactly are you?"

"Buddy Steel."

"What can we do for you, Mr. Steel?"

"Sheriff Steel."

"Sheriff?"

"Of San Remo County."

"Shouldn't you be wearing some kind of uniform? You know, by way of identification?"

"I have an aversion to uniforms."

She exchanged glances with the shaggy-haired man.

"Please forgive us. We were expecting someone else. I'm Pippa Rosin and this is my husband, James."

I nodded to each of them.

James Rosin leaned forward. "What brings you here, Sheriff Steel?"

"My never-ending quest for information."

"What kind of information?"

"You're listed as the ad agency for the Heart of Our Saviour Ministry."

Rosin glanced at his wife, then at me. "That's correct."

"Is this a bad time?"

"A bad time for what?"

"A chat."

Again Rosin looked at his wife. "I'm sorry," he said. "You must think us terribly rude. Please have a seat."

"A seat would be good."

Rosin pointed to the two visitors' chairs in front of his desk. I sat. Pippa sat beside me.

"May we offer you anything?" Pippa asked.

"Thank you, no."

"A Coke? Some coffee?"

"I'm good, thank you."

James sat back in his comfortable-looking armchair. "Okay," he said, "shoot."

"You do the Ministry's advertising?"

"We do."

"What exactly does that entail?"

James smiled. "Ordinarily, we prepare whatever ads the Ministry might require for the promotion of any of their events. For instance, we created the ad campaign for the upcoming Heart of Our Saviour Celebration. We devised multimedia spots and promos to appear on television and in print."

"Commercials."

"You might call them commercials, although we much prefer to refer to them as media messages."

I nodded. "Can you tell me where can I see these media messages?"

Rosin looked at Pippa. After several moments, he said, "We're expecting them to begin appearing shortly."

"You mean I can't see them now?"

"That's correct."

"Doesn't the Celebration take place next week?"

"It does."

"Forgive my ignorance, but don't media ad campaigns generally begin appearing well in advance of the actual event?"

"Normally they do, yes."

"And this one?"

"This one's an anomaly," James said.

"In what way?"

Neither of them said anything. They exchanged glances.

"Am I missing something here?"

"The ad campaign can't begin airing until the commercial time is paid for."

"Like eating in a fast-food restaurant."

"Excuse me?"

"You pay before you eat."

James smiled. "Something like that, yes."

"So what you're saying is the airtime hasn't yet been paid for."

"That's what I'm saying, yes."

"May I ask a dumb question?"

"Feel free."

"Why?"

"Why what?"

"Why hasn't the ad space been paid for?"

"That's a good question."

"Do you have a good answer?"

"That's the point. We don't have any answer."

"I'm going to assume you've billed the Ministry for the cost of the space."

"We have."

"And they haven't paid you?"

"Correct."

I didn't say anything.

James took a deep breath. "May I speak candidly, Sheriff Steel?"

"I would certainly hope so."

"The actual campaign began airing two months ago. As per the pre-approved media plan. We opened with a blitz. We peppered the airways and the print media with Celebration advertisements. We also bought a quarter of a million dollars' worth of television time. We advanced the funds for these buys. Exactly as we had done in years past. We've had a long relationship with the Ministry, so we made the buy on its behalf and then billed them for it."

"And they didn't pay."

"We didn't become alarmed until our second billing went unanswered. We're a small agency and don't have the assets to cover the sizable amount we fronted."

"What did they say?"

"You mean the Ministry?"

"Yes."

"That's just it. They didn't say anything. They never responded. Our reserves were quickly exhausted. We were forced to lay off our staff. We're now looking at possibly closing the agency."

"Did you tell this to anyone at the Ministry?"

"We told it to everyone at the Ministry. Those who would speak with us, that is. We were never able to make contact with either the Reverend or his brother."

"Hickey."

"Yes. Hickey was our principal contact."

"And he refused to take your calls."

"Not only that," Pippa said, "when James showed up at his office unannounced, he refused to see him. He sneaked out a back door, the son of a bitch."

"So what happens now?"

"God only knows. We've spoken with a lawyer, but without assets, we're unable to afford his fee. We're trying to raise enough money to cover it."

"Wouldn't this be an open-and-shut case?"

"You'd think," Pippa said. "But without a signed authorization to spend the money on the Ministry's behalf, the lawyer said there's no assurance we would successfully retrieve our loss."

"Yikes."

"Yikes, indeed," James said.

The three of us sat in silence for a while.

"Why do you think they didn't pay you?"

"Although it's hard to believe," Pippa said, "I think they're experiencing some kind of financial meltdown."

"You know, someone else told me there were rumors they were delinquent in paying their suppliers."

"You mean it's endemic?"

"It might be."

The Rosins sat silently for a while.

"Shit," James said.

"Exactly," I echoed.

Chapter Sixteen

Marsha Russo stuck her head into my office and bel-lowed, "Show time."

I looked at my watch. "I don't get it."

"What don't you get?"

"This whole thing. I don't understand what happened to Catharine Long. I can't figure out why they're having financial issues. None of it makes sense."

"Ours is not to reason why…"

"That's very helpful, Marsha."

"What do you think is going on?"

"I'm totally clueless."

"What else is new?"

"There is one thing."

I caught Marsha's response from the corner of my eye. "I knew I should have gotten out when the getting was good."

"When Reverend Barry was attempting to throw us off the scent, he said that Catharine was with his sister. Why don't we *cherchez la femme?*"

"I beg your pardon?"

"See if you can locate the sister. Margaret, right?"

Marsha nodded.

"And while you're at it, indulge me a little."

"This is even worse than I imagined. Indulge you, how?"

"I want to know if any of these clowns have priors."

"I presume you're referring to Barry, Barry, and Hickham."

"Correct."

"And you want to know if any of them have a record."

"Correct again."

"And you want me to look into it."

"You catch on fast."

She smiled. "Years of practice."

Chapter Seventeen

Eight police cruisers convened about a mile from the Long estate, accompanied by a Lenco BearCat Counter-Attack truck, complete with a battering-ram attachment, for use if necessary.

A light rain was falling when I gave the signal. I pulled out and led the procession to the main entrance, where I pressed the call button. It was quickly answered.

"Long residence," a male voice responded.

"This is County Sheriff Buddy Steel. Please open the gate."

There was only silence.

"Are you still there? Did you hear me?"

"I'm sorry. I'm alone here. I have no authority to let you in."

"I'm in possession of a search warrant signed by Judge Ezekiel Azenberg. Please open the gate."

After several moments, the voice said, "I can't do that."

"Should you continue to ignore my request, I'll have no choice but to ram the gate."

"May I at least see the warrant?"

"You may."

"I'll come right down."

The intercom went silent.

We waited.

In short order, a young man came walking swiftly down the driveway. I got out of my cruiser and waited for him to arrive at the gate.

As he approached, I saw that it was the same young man who had greeted us on our first visit. I handed him the warrant through the bars of the gate.

"It's Jeffrey, right?"

The man started and peered at me. "It is," he said. "Thank you for remembering. Hardly anyone does." He waved the warrant. "How do I know this is authentic?"

"Because I say it is."

"And if I don't open the gate?"

"Do you see the BearCat behind me? The one with the battering ram?"

Jeffrey took note of the Bear Cat, his spirits visibly sinking.

"That's the alternative."

"You mean you'd barge your way in."

"In a manner of speaking."

Jeffrey stepped to the gate and punched in four numbers. The gate slid open. He moved back to allow the convoy to proceed.

I felt sorry for him, out of his league and over his head. "Get in. I'll drive you up to the house."

Jeffrey shrugged and climbed into my cruiser. I waved the BearCat off and proceeded up the winding driveway.

"What's this about?" he asked.

"We're going to execute a search of the premises."

"They'll make me pay for this."

"For what?"

"For letting you onto the property. Hickey will go bat shit."

"I presume he's at the Pavilion."

"They're all at the Pavilion. Except me and Milton. And the maids."

"Milton?"

"The estate manager."

"Where is Milton now?"

"Somewhere out on the grounds."

"Where?"

"I wouldn't know. He could be anywhere."

The procession arrived in front of the big house and parked in the motor court. No other vehicles were there.

I stepped out and called to Johnny Kennerly who had emerged from one of the other cruisers. "Let the games begin."

Johnny raised his arm and seven officers scurried across the porch and into the house.

"Where did you last see him?" I asked Jeffrey.

"Milton?"

"Yes."

"I saw him at breakfast."

"And since then?"

"I don't know where he is."

I motioned to Al Striar, who was standing nearby. "Find Milton. Jeffrey here will direct you."

I turned back to the young man. "This is Deputy Striar. Perhaps you could assist him."

Nervous, Jeffrey began shifting his weight from foot to foot. "I'll do my best."

"What exactly is it you do here, Jeffrey? Other than answer the doorbell, that is."

"I'm an intern. I was selected from among more than five hundred applicants."

"Very impressive. What is it an intern does around here?"

"Lots of things. What I like best is working on the TV productions.

He smiled. I noticed anew his mouthful of oversized, glimmering teeth.

"Do you whiten them?"

"Excuse me?"

"Your teeth. Have they been whitened?"

"No, sir. They've always been like that."

"Amazing."

My tongue unconsciously poked around my own teeth in search of any potential cavities. "You're lucky."

"Genes."

"Luck," I countered.

Chapter Eighteen

The investigation began on the top floor. I joined the search team, which included Johnny Kennerly, Marsha Russo, and P.J. Lincoln.

The entire floor had been converted into a sort of dormitory, presumably for the resident staff. Ten rooms, five to a side, were separated by a narrow hallway, accessible only by a single staircase. Each room was painted in antique white and contained a bed, dresser, desk, two lamps, and an armchair. Not all of them appeared to be occupied.

The dormitory's sloping ceilings were low, barely allowing room for a person to stand. Only a few had windows. Separate bathrooms for men and women were located at both ends of the hallway.

The occupants were present in two of the rooms. They were young women in their early twenties, each terrified by our presence. Both wore traditional housemaid's uniforms. Neither spoke English.

I instructed P.J. Lincoln to find Raul Ybanez, one of the two Latino members of the San Remo Sheriff's

Department, and summon him to the mansion so he might interview the two women.

I wandered through the other rooms and found five that were lived in. I guessed they belonged to the security staff, most of whom had likely accompanied the Reverend to Long Pavilion. I tasked P.J. with inventorying the rooms and gleaning as much information as he could about the residents.

The floor below consisted of four separate suites, each opening onto a large and airy U-shaped landing that stood at the head of a grand staircase. Oversized casement windows provided natural light as well as ocean vistas.

Three matching crystal chandeliers hung in a line from the fifteen-foot-high ceiling. Groupings of ornate furniture were arranged on the landing. Gold-framed Western-style paintings adorned the walls.

The master suite included a large bedroom, double-sized bathroom, two adjoining dressing rooms, and an exercise room containing a treadmill, two stationary bikes, and a weight machine.

There was also a family room with a wall-mounted, wide-screen TV, a half-sized refrigerator, two coffee-makers, and a microwave.

I wandered around, searching for anything that might resemble a clue.

A child's room held a single bed upon which rested a pair of stuffed animals. A bedside table had on it a copy of Margaret Wise Smith and Clement Hurd's picture book, *Goodnight Moon*. A tricycle stood in the center of the richly carpeted floor.

There was a no-frills room with a queen bed and a

bureau, on top of which were two photographs, one a close-up of little Barry III mugging for the camera, and the other a shot of an elderly man on whose lap the boy was seated. Young Three was all smiles, but the old man's eyes projected a vacant stare. I guessed he was Catharine's father.

An armchair and a reading lamp stood in a corner beneath a dormer window. A pile of books sat on a side table; the topmost of which was Gillian Flynn's *Gone Girl*. I presumed this was Catharine's room.

I nosed through her closet, which held a neatly arranged wardrobe of dresses, skirts, jackets, various styles of slacks, jeans, and colorful tops. Two rows of fashionable shoes and sneakers were lined up in racks on the floor. An adjoining black-and-white-tiled bathroom was antiseptically clean. A wall-mounted cabinet held nothing out of the ordinary. Apart from a small jar of Advil, there were no medicines.

I stood silently for a while. The room revealed little of the woman who occupied it, except for the possibility that she slept apart from her husband.

I stepped into the exercise room. A towel was draped over the handlebar of one of the stationary bikes. Gym shorts and a wrinkled tee-shirt hung on a hook just outside the adjoining bathroom with twin sinks, a stall shower with six water spigots, a bidet, a high-rise toilet, and a large whirlpool bathtub.

The master bedroom featured a California king bed beneath a teak canopy frame, each side of which was adorned with hand-painted Japanese silk netting.

Dormer windows and double French doors opened onto a glassed-in patio and its pair of upholstered deck chairs, two cafe umbrellas, and a sensational view of the Pacific. A retractable ceiling exposed the room to the sun and salt air whenever desired.

A sitting area in the bedroom held a love seat, a coffee table, and a pair of leather armchairs. There was also a large walk-in closet, the size of a small country.

In addition to rows upon rows of hanging clothing, the closet contained a built-in mahogany bureau that stretched its entire length. A small chair and floor lamp occupied one of its corners.

One of the rows was devoted solely to blue jeans and work shirts. There were at least twenty pairs of starched jeans and a greater number of long-sleeved denim shirts. These were the Reverend's work costumes. On a separate rack hung his designer suits, sport jackets, and slacks.

I rummaged through bureau drawers filled with dress shirts, sport shirts, sweaters, underwear, short- and long-sleeved tee-shirts, socks, sweatshirts, sweatpants, and track suits. Dozens of dress shoes, loafers, sneakers, and assorted footwear filled shoe racks.

The only other items that caught my eye were located in one of the bottom drawers of the bureau. There I found jars of personal lubricants, condoms in varying styles, and several vials of performance-enhancing medications. There was also a collection of pornographic videos.

"Looks like our Reverend has a taste for the hinky," I murmured to myself.

I was just leaving the suite when Johnny Kennerly came rushing up the stairs.

"Buddy." He was slightly out of breath. "I found something you need to see."

Chapter Nineteen

I followed Johnny downstairs, through the kitchen and into a small pantry, inside of which stood a heavy wooden door, sealed shut by a pair of deadbolt locks.

"This is it," he said.

"The locked door."

"Yes."

"Why?"

"It's strange. There's a door on the far side of the kitchen that leads to the basement. It's unlocked and accessible. It's a pretty large basement. But I can't figure out where this door leads. And why it's double-bolted."

"Our master key doesn't fit?"

"No."

"You're sure?"

"I'm sure."

"Okay."

"Okay what?"

"Let's blow the sucker."

I unholstered my Colt Commander and shot. "Fire in the hole," I shouted.

Johnny stood back and covered his ears. I fired two shots, each disabling one of the deadbolts. The noise was considerable.

"That ought to do it."

Once down the stairs behind the door, we found ourselves standing in a large chamber that contained three prison cells, each with a heavy metal door into which a small barred window had been implanted. The door to one of the cells hung open.

I stepped inside. It was small and windowless, disagreeably musty and dank-smelling. It held a cot bed and a single canvas armchair. A toilet stood in one of the corners. A sink hung on the opposite wall. The cot was made up with two sheets and a brown woolen blanket. There were no visible traces of anyone having recently occupied it.

"What do you think?" Johnny asked, looking around.

"Why would anyone have three jail cells in their basement?"

"It's weird."

"Beyond weird."

"Maybe they were constructed before the Long family moved in."

"Maybe," I said, "but why would the cells be so well maintained? Why is the bed freshly made?"

"So what do you want to do?"

"Before this scene becomes polluted, I want a forensics team in here. I want to learn whether Catharine Long was ever in any of these cells. I want them to examine the wood, the concrete, the fixtures and determine how old they are. That should tell us if the Longs had them built."

"And then what?"

"We abide the events."

From the top of the stairs, Al Striar called down to us. "Buddy?"

"Yep."

"Milton's waiting in the kitchen."

He was a large man in his middle years, two hundred-plus pounds, with a slouchy posture and tobacco-stained teeth.

He had big features, a bulbous nose, oversized ears, large lips, and huge hands. He wore a bleached work shirt tucked into stained overalls. Around his waist was a service belt on which were attached weathered tools, including a hammer, several screwdrivers, and a heavy-duty wrench.

He was enveloped in a cloud of malevolence.

"Your name is…?"

"Milton Pfenster," he said.

"Fenster with an 'F' or Phenster with a 'Ph'?"

"With a 'Pf'. But the 'P' is silent."

"What is it you do here, Mr. Pfenster?"

"Mostly handy work. General repairs. Stuff like that."

"Are you aware of the three cells that exist in the basement of the house?"

"Yes."

"Is it your job to service those cells?"

"Service them?

"Clean them. Maintain them. Stuff like that."

"No."

"So, mostly you're restricted to the outside of the house, is that correct?"

"Mostly. Yes."

"But you know the Longs."

"Somewhat."

"Do you know Catharine Long?"

"She says hello to me."

"Do you know where she is?"

"You mean now?"

"Yes."

"No, sir."

"Were you ever present during one of their fights?"

"What fights? You mean Reverend and Mrs. Long?"

"Yes."

"I never saw no fights. I never saw much of anything going on in the house. Like I said, I'm mostly an outdoors person. I make sure the landscaping is up to snuff. I look out for the cars. I check the perimeter. That kind of stuff."

"Nothing regarding the actual house?"

"Plumbing sometimes. Heating. Stuff like that. Oh, yeah. And the swimming pool, too."

"You live here?"

"On the grounds, you mean?"

"Yes."

"I do. There's a small cottage down near the stables that's mine. I mean, I don't own it or nothing. I just live in it."

"I see. Thank you for time, Mr...."

"Pfenster."

'That's right. Pfenster."

"Milton Pfenster."

"The 'P' is silent," I said.

We stood awkwardly for several moments.

Then I asked, "Military?"

"'Nam. Persian Gulf."

"Rank?"

"Staff Sergeant."

"Thank you for your service, Sergeant Pfenster."

"That's kind of you, Sheriff. Most people couldn't care less."

After he left, I summoned Al Striar.

"I want to know everything there is to know about Staff Sergeant Milton Pfenster."

"I'm all over it," Striar said.

"I even want to know why the 'P' is silent."

Striar flashed me his dead-eyed stare.

I returned it with one of my own, and said, "Just kidding."

Chapter Twenty

"The Hart Building," Marsha said.

I was heading back to the station in my cruiser. "What about it?"

"It's on Third and Lucy. In the financial district."

"So?"

"It's home to Long & Long Financial Services, Inc."

"Barry Long?"

"Senior. And Hickham Long."

"What's the exact address?"

"1013 Lucy."

"Got it. Thanks."

"What are you going to do?"

"Have a look."

"Don't do anything foolish, Buddy."

I clicked off the call and concentrated on finding the Hart Building.

Lucy Street turned out to be more of an oversized alleyway than a legitimate thoroughfare. I found number 1013, and parked at a meter.

The building was an example of the International style of architecture, constructed in the early 1940s and molded mostly from what were then considered modern materials—concrete, glass, and steel. It was more utilitarian than artful, more serviceable than aesthetically pleasing.

I entered the flat-roofed building and climbed the stairs to the second floor where I found a highly polished American cedar door that bore the legend, *Long & Long, Inc.,* in gold serif letters. A gold-rimmed spy hole was cut into the door. A bell and speaker were carved into the frame.

I rang the bell.

"Yes," a disembodied male voice responded.

"Is this Barry Long's office?"

"These are the offices of Long and Long."

"Inc."

"Excuse me?"

"The sign on the door says Long and Long, Inc."

After several moments, the buzzer sounded and the door popped open.

I was greeted by a nerdy young man wearing an inexpensive, ill-fitting seersucker suit. He peered at me through the thick horn-rimmed glasses that dominated the upper half of his face. The glasses rested on an aquiline nose above a pair of pencil thin lips. "What can I do for you?" he asked.

"I'm looking for Barry Long, Senior."

"And you are?"

"Buddy Steel."

"Does Mr. Long know you?"

"He does not."

"Do you have an appointment?"

"No."

"You're out of luck, then."

"Meaning?"

"He's not here."

"When do you expect him?"

"I wouldn't know."

"Would you mind if I waited?"

"Do what you want, Jack, but we close at five."

"Is he likely to be back before then?"

"I just got finished telling you I don't know when, or even if, he'll be back."

"What are the odds?"

"The odds?"

"The relative probability of the event occurring."

"I know the definition of odds."

"So, what are they?"

"You know what, pal? I don't think I like you."

"Everyone says that."

"Why don't we just agree that Mr. Long isn't coming back today and leave it at that?"

"But what if he did?"

"Did what?"

"Come back."

"Then you wouldn't be here to see him, would you?"

"Not unless I chose to wait."

"If you did that, you'd be waiting outside. You're no longer welcome here."

"I get a lot of that, too."

"Well, you got it again."

The man opened the door and held it for me.

"May I leave my card?"

"I don't think so. Mr. Long won't want to see you."

"Without even knowing what it's about?"

"Out," the man said.

I gave him my most fearsome look. "Tell him Sheriff Steel was here to see him."

"Sheriff?"

"That's right."

"If you're a Sheriff, why aren't you wearing a uniform?"

"Because I don't like them."

"Yeah, right. Whatever. Leave."

"Are you always this pleasant?"

"Only to non-uniformed Sheriffs."

He pointed me to the door and slammed it closed behind me. Once outside, I heard the tumbler click and the lock fall into place.

Chapter Twenty-one

Wilma followed me into my office carrying a handful of phone messages.

"Let me guess," I said. "Alfred Wilder and Her Honor. Not necessarily in that order."

"I'll bet you made number one on each of their speed dials."

"The big-time, at last."

Alfred "Skip" Wilder picked up my call immediately.

"It's a shit storm here," he said.

"I hope you're wearing boots."

"Don't start, Buddy. Lytell's livid. He's already phoned half the judges in the building trying to find out who authorized the warrant."

"Azenberg."

"What?"

"Ezekiel Azenberg. He authorized it."

"This is serious, Buddy. The Long family is threatening to sue."

"Sue who?"

"San Remo County. You."

"A fearsome turn of events."

"For you, it might well be."

"Listen, Skip. We were well within our rights to seek the warrant. There's a whole lot of strangeness going on."

"Such as?"

"The disappearance of Catharine Long, for openers."

"The family denies that claim."

"Then why don't they show her to us?"

"They're claiming your investigation is an invasion of their privacy."

"Like hell it is. Has anyone called your attention to the money issues?"

"What money issues?"

"The Longs are stiffing their suppliers."

"Meaning?"

"The Ministry has stopped paying its bills."

"Over what period of time?"

"Several months."

"Maybe they're on an extended pay schedule."

"And maybe pigs fly."

"What did your raid produce?"

"They've got three prison cells in the basement."

"So?"

"Forensics is examining the DNA to determine whether Catharine may have been held in any of them."

"Forensics might be able to determine whether or not she was in a cell, but they'll never prove she was held there against her will."

I listened as Wilder's alleged outrage turned smug.

"You've got nothing, Buddy. I know it. Lytell knows it. Murray Kornbluth knows it and he's gunning for you. He doesn't much like you and he's planning to take you down a few notches."

"I'm shaking like a leaf. All he has to do is produce Catharine."

"It's not going to happen. Kornbluth is saying she's got emotional issues."

"That's a load of crap."

I took Wilder's silence as insinuation the conversation had come to its end.

"I'm not done, Skip."

"When Lytell sticks his fork in you, you will be."

"Meaning?"

"You and me, Buddy. We've been friends since high school. I'm very concerned about what this might cost you."

"I'll take my chances. This fish stinks from the head and I intend to prove it."

"Don't say I didn't warn you."

Wilder ended the call.

Chapter Twenty-two

I was shown into the private dining room of the investment banking firm Elliot J. Goldman, LLC, one of California's top financial institutions, handling nearly a billion dollars of client assets.

Its chairman, Billy Goldman, son of the late founder, stood to greet me when I entered. The dining room was on the main floor of the converted town house in which Goldman lived, and also served as the Freedom adjunct of the company's sprawling banking and trading facility that was located in San Remo City.

Goldman was an elegantly attired, handsomely coiffed gentleman in his late sixties, who appeared to have been spawned in an age when good manners and civility counted for something. Everything about him boasted of proper breeding, understated elegance, and, of course, money.

I had met Billy Goldman in my youth. His home had suffered a break-in and a number of his personal treasures, including a pair of Picasso drawings, had been stolen.

My father played a key role in locating those items and bringing the thieves to justice. I frequently accompanied him in those days and was witness to how he solved the crime and earned the Goldman family's trust and friendship.

Billy pointed me to the chair across from him at the smartly laid, linen-covered table set for two.

"Thank you for seeing me here," Goldman said. "I have to admit that I rarely leave the premises these days. I hardly ever get to San Remo. The older I become, the less mobile I am. By choice. Comes with the territory, I suppose."

An unobtrusive butler stepped quietly to the table and poured steaming hot coffee from a silver pot into my gilt-edged Lenox china cup. He placed a tray of sweeteners and a pitcher of milk in front of me. He offered a glass of freshly squeezed orange juice, which I accepted gratefully.

"It's nice to see you again, Buddy," Goldman said. "I've been hearing some unfortunate rumblings about the state of Burton's health. Is there any truth to them?"

"Unfortunately, there is."

"Gehrig's?"

"Yes."

"I'm sorry. How is he doing?"

"He's a fighter."

"Always was. Will you send him my regards?

"He'll be pleased."

Goldman nodded. "What brings you?"

"My never-ending search for truth and justice."

"How unusual."

"In this instance, you're the only person I know who might possess it."

"The information you're seeking?"

"Yes."

"Might I inquire as to what that might be?"

"Are you familiar with the Long family?"

"You mean the Barry Long family?"

"I do."

"Amazing," Goldman said.

"What's amazing?"

"Either you're prescient or you're in the know."

"In the know about what?"

The butler entered carrying a pair of dishes, each covered with a sterling silver lid. He placed one in front of me and the other in front of Billy. He removed the lids with a flourish, revealing plates filled with scrambled eggs topped by shredded cheddar cheese and scallion slivers, accompanied by generous portions of home-fried potatoes. He also put small serving pitchers containing catsup and hot sauce in the center of the table. After receiving a signal from Billy Goldman, the butler quietly slipped out of the room.

"Please start," Goldman said.

"It looks wonderful. Generally, I breakfast on burnt coffee and stale donuts."

"Ah, the policeman's special."

"Exactly."

"Hopefully, you'll derive a larger measure of nutrition from this breakfast."

"Hopefully, my system can handle it."

Goldman smiled and dug in.

"What were you saying about being prescient?"

"There's a disturbing buzz on the street."

Goldman wiped a small piece of egg from the corner of his mouth. "It has to do in part with the Long family."

"Meaning?"

"Have you ever come in contact with Oliver Darien?"

"Not that I recall."

"Darien and Company?"

I shook my head.

"Ollie Darien is one of life's great conundrums. He built one of the most talked-about investment broker-ages on the West Coast. He handles untold amounts for loyal clients who swear by him and his results. He manages to top the market averages on a regular basis. He accepts clients only by invitation. He's made himself into a living legend."

"And?"

"Does this description put you in mind of anyone else?"

"Bernard Madoff?"

"Bingo. Can I swear you to secrecy, Buddy?"

"You already know the answer, Billy."

"There's a rumor flying around that Ollie Darien is about to be indicted."

"For?"

"Ponzi scheming."

"Like Madoff?"

"Exactly like Madoff. And, in all likelihood, with the same results."

"Meaning?"

"A tremendous loss of presumed wealth for his clients."

"How does this affect the Long family?"

"Barry Long, Senior, is Ollie Darien's closest friend."

"So?"

"It's being whispered that Barry, Senior, invested every penny he and his family own with Ollie. Not only his cash assets, but it's also rumored he converted all of his real estate holdings into cash and forked that over to Ollie as well."

"Leaving him with?"

"A headache the size of Montana. He's ruined. Once it becomes public, every so-called friend and donor will be out the door quicker than a Clayton Kershaw fastball."

"Are you sure about this?"

"Reasonably sure."

"Why hasn't it been made public?"

"The Justice Department is insistent upon verifying every possible allegation. We're hearing they're days away from announcing."

"You're sure about Senior Long?"

"He's scrambling, Buddy. As I mentioned, the word is already on the street. Senior Long, as you refer to him, is trying to dump as much of his Darien holdings as he can."

"And?"

"The buzz is ahead of him. He's gotten no takers. He's fucked."

"Yikes."

"Exactly."

"What happens to him?"

"Armageddon is what happens to him. And to his family."

"Despite the funds that the ministry brings in?"

"You can only imagine how his flock will react when they learn how cavalier The People's Pastor has been with the people's money. It's one thing to give it away, it's another to piss it away."

"You think the spigot will run dry?"

"I do."

"Because?"

"Once faith is breached, it's damned near impossible to regain."

"What's the best they can hope for?"

"That the news doesn't break before their annual Celebration."

"Can that happen?"

"You mean can the Justice Department be persuaded to hold the story?"

"Yes."

"It's possible. You never know in whose pocket any Washingtonian resides."

"So what's next?"

"We wait and see. But one way or the other, it's still *Adios*, Barry."

"Meaning?"

"The harder they fall..." Goldman said.

Chapter Twenty-three

"Bingo," Marsha Russo exclaimed when I returned her voice message.

"Do you think you could you be more explicit?"

"Hickham Long."

I waited.

"Grand larceny."

"He stole something?"

"A Rolex."

"He stole a watch?"

"A very pricey watch."

"From?"

"Nordstrom, the department store."

"Where and when?"

"Glendale, California. June, 2000."

"When he was how old?"

"Just nineteen."

"And he was charged?"

"He barely made the age cut, but yes, he was."

"And?"

"Bailed out by his old man."

"But the charges are still on the books."

"They are. Glendale police even had the gloves he wore during the holdup."

"Bingo, indeed. Anything on the others?"

"You mean Barry and/or Barry?"

"Yes."

"Nothing on either."

"Just Hickey."

"Just him. Yes."

We were silent until Marsha spoke again. "I inquired as to whether Glendale might lend us the gloves. I suggested we'd like to run some matching DNA tests."

"And?"

"They arrived by special courier."

"You mean you have the gloves?"

"Yep. They're calfskin. Like *buttah*."

"Why would they do that?"

"You mean send us the gloves?"

"Yes."

"Two possible reasons."

"Which are?"

"Well for openers, they like me. They really like me."

"And the second reason?"

"The case was cleared long ago. The Glendale police officer was surprised they still had the records, never mind the evidence bags. They were happy to send them. Otherwise they were likely to toss them."

"Where are they now?"

"Waiting in a safe place."

"Waiting for what?"

"To match a sample of Hickham Long's DNA in an incriminating context. That's what you want, isn't it?"

"I never said that."

"But you're hoping that sooner or later it will."

"Better sooner."

"Better never."

"What's that supposed to mean?"

"I know you have a jones for this guy, Buddy. From that day at his brother's house. But this whole Long thing is loaded."

"Loaded with?"

"Stuff you don't even know about. These bozos are lawyered up and they have considerable juice."

"So you're suggesting…"

"I'm not suggesting anything. All I'm saying is that sometimes it's better to let sleeping dogs lie. I'd hate to see this puppy jump up and bite you in the ass."

"Duly noted," I said. "Thank you."

Chapter Twenty-four

"Sounds like you have yourself one fine mess," my father said.

He and I were sitting in his study in the late afternoon. Glints of reflected sunlight projected off the roiling sea.

"Not nearly as big as the mess the Long family has gotten itself into."

"Meaning?"

"Apart from the missing Catharine, it appears as if Barry, Senior, has lost everything."

"What everything?"

"Every penny they own."

"How could that be possible?"

"Ask Billy Goldman, who sends you his regards, by the way."

"He knows I'm ill?"

"He knows everything about everyone."

"He does, doesn't he? What does he say happened to the Longs?"

"You know Oliver Darien?"

"Know of."

"Seems he's pulled a Madoff,"

"He ran a Ponzi scheme?"

"Broke the old man's bank."

"Barry, Senior?"

"He's the surrogate for the whole shebang."

"Jesus."

We sat quietly for a while.

"I haven't been able to penetrate the facade," I said.

"What do you mean?"

"My initial plan was to break into Long Pavilion with guns blazing but I'm guessing that's not a winning tactic."

"Not hardly."

"Forensics confirms that Catharine Long was in one of the basement cells but there's no way to establish whether or not she was there of her own volition."

"You think she camped out in one of those cells by choice?"

"I didn't say that."

"Where do you think she is?"

"Well, we know she's not at the house. And I'd bet they wouldn't be foolish enough to have stashed her at the Pavilion."

"But you're not sure."

"I'm not. Too many mixed messages. Reverend Barry told us she was with his sister."

"His sister?"

"Yes. We've yet to determine the sister's whereabouts so we can't confirm the Reverend's statement. But we do know that if they are together, it's not where he told us they were. And to further complicate matters, Murray Kornbluth claims he's seen her but won't tell us where."

"*Upright and Uptight* Kornbluth?"

"One and the same. He can't have made such a claim without being able to back it up. He's an officer of the court, after all."

Burton smiled, conscious of how prone Kornbluth was to creating conflicts of interest regarding court-related issues and his own personal ones, and how he always managed to skate on all of them.

I snapped him out of his reverie. "There's also no way of knowing where he saw her and what condition she was in when he did."

"What do you think?"

"Damned if I know. It's all curious. Maybe she learned about the precarious nature of her family's finances and, realizing she was standing on the unexpected threshold of financial ruin, she might have come unhinged."

"Meaning?"

"God knows what she might be capable of doing, but from what little I know about her, having it out with her husband wouldn't be an unlikely scenario."

"So you think they fought."

"According to what the nanny said, they were fighting regularly."

"And you think he became violent with her?"

"I can't figure him out. His veneer is as smooth as a baby's ass, but there's something unnerving about him. Did he really abdicate his finances to his father and brother? Did he know about the financial cliff they were going over?

"And just who is this father, anyway, and what kind of relationship do the two of them have? If what Billy

Goldman said is true, and Senior Long is the architect of their economic calamity, what's he doing about it and what's his state of mind? All that aside, however, the question still remains, where's Catharine?"

"So, how do you answer that question?"

"I wish I knew."

"How unlike you."

"I'm still at square one. The lawyers are stonewalling me. I have questions but no answers. If I don't come up with something soon, I'm likely to be shown the door. Which could impact you."

"You think?"

"It's dicey."

"Let me tell you something, Buddy. You're doing the right thing. You're doing what needs to be done. These other clowns, Kornbluth, Lytell, Long Senior…they're all in cahoots with their own self interests. Fuck 'em. You do what you have to do and fuck 'em all."

"That's your advice?"

"Rendered free of charge, too."

Chapter Twenty-five

"We found her," Marsha said.

She had phoned me in my cruiser. "Found who?"

"The sister."

"Where?"

"Los Angeles. She goes by the name Maggie de Winter."

"de Winter?"

"Yes."

"Married name?"

"Wasn't specified."

"How did you find her?"

"I'm very good at my job."

"No one's questioning that, Marsha. Still, how did you find her?"

"Will it be our little secret?"

I sighed. "Why does this have to be so hard?"

"Google."

"Excuse me?"

"I Googled her. I also used Instant Checkmate. The trail led to Maggie de Winter."

"Is it accurate?"

"You mean is a Google search accurate?"

"Yes."

"Of course it's accurate. What century are you living in?"

"You're certain she's the sister?"

"I am."

"How?"

"How what?"

"How can you be certain?"

"She told me."

"Who told you?"

"She did. I phoned her."

"You phoned her?"

"Stop repeating everything I say. Yes, I phoned her."

"And she answered?"

"No, the Pope answered. But he put me straight through to her. She confirmed her identity."

"To you."

"Of course to me."

"Why would she confirm her identity to you?"

"Because I told her I was from Publisher's Clearing House. I said she was a winner."

"And so believing she had won some kind of prize, she made assurances to you that she was Maggie de Winter, nee Margaret Long."

"Yes."

"What did you do then?"

"I hung up."

"You what?"

"I hung up. I had the information I needed. I saw no reason to carry on the conversation. Aren't you proud of me?"

"In an odd way, I suppose I am."

"Well, la di dah," she said.

"Marsha?"

"Yes."

"Thank you."

"You're welcome."

"Did you get her address?"

"I already had it."

"Google?"

"Instant Checkmate."

"Did you confirm it?"

"Yes."

"Good work, Marsha."

"I'm just a cacophony of good work these days."

"Try not to let it go to your head," I told her and ended the call.

Chapter Twenty-six

I hadn't been in Los Angeles since I'd moved back to Freedom. Upon entering the city limits, I suffered an unexpected twinge of nostalgia.

I exited the 101 Freeway at Vine Street and went south, passing the Capitol Records building and the Pantages Theatre before turning onto Hollywood Boulevard at Raymond Chandler Square where I drove past Fredrick's of Hollywood, Madame Tussauds Wax Museum, and on to Grauman's Chinese Theatre, where I spotted Wonder Woman and Batman hustling the tourists.

I made my way east on Sunset Boulevard and drove past the Cinerama Dome, The Hollywood Palladium, and the Henry Fonda, a jewel box of a theatre that originally brought honor to the memory of the great actor for whom it was named, but which was now a seedy rock 'n' roll emporium.

I turned onto Cahuenga Boulevard, spotted the Los Angeles Fire Department Museum and pulled into the parking lot it shared with the Hollywood Community

Police headquarters where I had been stationed during my time as an LAPD homicide detective.

I parked in front, content to simply sit there for a few minutes, fascinated by the comings and goings of the station, and those of the ramshackle bail bondsman's office located directly across the street.

This was the part of L.A. I knew, two short blocks from the apartment building where I'd lived, an anachronistic relic of the movie town's golden era, now newly restored and part of a resurgent Hollywood with its mélange of shops, restaurants, and theatres, plus the Hollywood Health Club, where I had spent almost all of my downtime.

As a result of its proximity to a phalanx of movie and TV studios, as well as a proliferation of major production entities, this burgeoning area had become home to show business upstarts, aspiring young people attracted to the new Hollywood with its low-cost housing and its high-profile history. Like me, many of them frequented the Health Club, all of us devoted to working out and hooking up.

In hindsight, I realize that living here was a happy time in my life. Happiness, not as a passing change of emphasis, but as a constant condition. It was here I savored my self-made success and the shared esteem of colleagues and friends.

Sitting as I was now, in the heart of my once-cherished neighborhood, I understood how much I missed it, and how much I yearned to return to it. As Randy Newman so famously sang, "I Love L.A."

I took one last look around, cranked up the Wrangler, turned right onto Sunset Boulevard and headed east.

Maggie de Winter lived in the Los Feliz section of L.A., the newly fashionable eastside neighborhood at the foot of Griffith Park.

She opened the door to her spacious apartment in the Towers, one of a pair of high-rise luxury buildings on Los Feliz Boulevard that offer panoramic views of Boyle Heights and the L.A. basin to the south, and the Hollywood Hills to the north.

She gave me the once-over, assessing me from head to toe, an unabashed consideration of my person coupled with a frank sexual appraisal.

I reciprocated.

"Sheriff, right?" she said.

"Close enough."

"Tall enough, too."

She stepped back to let me in. She was statuesque and leggy, narrow and lithe with proper curves in all the right places. She wore skin-tight black capri running pants, a yellow tank top, and red Nike sneakers. Her eyes were a deep blue. Her auburn hair fell in waves over her shoulders and she frequently brushed it away from her forehead. Hers was an aristocratic nose and I found it difficult to tear my eyes from her moist, sensuous lips. I was smitten, and she noticed.

She led me to her kitchen where she offered coffee and Social Tea biscuits. I sat at a Formica-topped table. She stood with her back against the sink, the Griffith Park Observatory visible through the picture window behind her.

"This is about my brother Barry, right?"

"Your sister-in-law, actually."

"Yes. That's what you said. I'm sorry. What is it about my sister-in-law that brings you all the way to L.A.?"

She swept the hair from her forehead.

I told her everything I knew.

She picked up her cup, carried it to the table and sat across from me.

"How tall exactly are you?"

"Six-three."

Once again the frankness of her gaze caught my attention and ennobled me to return it.

"Why would you think I have any knowledge of what might have happened to my sister-in-law?"

"Something your brother said."

"Which was?"

"He said she was staying with you."

"He lied."

"She's not staying with you?"

"Never has. Never will. I have very little contact with my family."

"Have you any idea why he would say such a thing?"

"I have no idea why my brother says or does anything. We don't get along."

"Because?"

"Why don't we just leave it at that."

She vanished into her thoughts for several moments. Then she returned and smiled at me.

"I guess it was a waste of time."

"What was?"

"Your visit to L.A."

"Not really. I wanted to get out of Freedom. The drive helped clear my head."

We sat quietly for a while.

"What is it you do here?" I asked.

"Would that be a Sheriff question or a personal one?"

"Personal."

She nodded. "Why?"

"Why what?"

"Why do you want to know?"

"What if I just want to extend my visit with you?"

"Do you?"

"Would you mind if I did?"

"Would you like to go for a walk?"

"Do you always answer a question with a question?"

"Why do you ask?"

She caught my grin and self-consciously whisked the hair from her forehead. "Where?"

"In the park?"

"Okay."

I stood. She stood close to me.

"You really are tall," she said.

"Is tall unusual?"

"For me it is."

"Because?"

"I'm six feet." She looked up at me. "I won't want to talk about my family."

"Okay."

"Do you want to know why?"

"Only if you want to tell me."

"Maybe on our walk."

Chapter Twenty-seven

We meandered up Hillhurst Avenue, which melded into Vermont Avenue, and two blocks later we were in the park. True to form, the Los Angeles weather was a knockout. The sun was high in a cloudless sky. The air was only slightly moist. We wandered in and out of the shade provided by ancient heritage oak, ficus, and dogwood trees. We circled the edge of a nine-hole golf course, passed half a dozen tennis courts, and strolled up a winding, pothole-pocked roadway that had long been closed to automobile traffic.

We found a wooden bench in a shady glen amidst a stand of towering pines and grabbed the chance to rest awhile, sitting side by side. Maggie gulped down water from a plastic thermos, then offered it to me. I took a large swallow.

"You're not afraid," she said.

"Of?"

"The consequences of investigating powerful people who wouldn't hesitate to come after you."

"Like members of your family?"

"I don't want to talk about my family."

"No."

"What, no?"

"I'm not intimidated by them."

"By my family."

"Yes."

She put the bottle to her lips and drank deeply.

"What is it you do?" I asked.

"About what?"

"About work."

"You mean do I have a job?"

"Yes."

"I'm an online reporter. A blogger."

"What do you blog?"

"I'm always on the lookout for socio-economic trends and I report on them. My goal is to get out in front of the next big thing and then advise my clients as to how they might capitalize on it."

"I have absolutely no understanding of what it is you just said."

"I'm a futurist, a prognosticator."

"Which means?"

"Do you know anything about social media?"

"No."

"No wonder you don't understand. You're a Luddite."

"And proud of it," I said. "Do you make great sums of money doing what you do?"

"Not hardly. The blog hasn't exactly caught fire yet. But my hopes remain high."

A sudden wind kicked up, blowing down through the hills, rustling the trees and stirring the air. A spot of debris caught me in the eye.

Maggie leaned closer to me and examined the eye, which had begun to tear up. She spotted the dirt speck. "Blink," she said.

"Excuse me?"

"Blink. Rapidly."

I did.

She pulled a Kleenex from her purse and as my tears intensified, she delicately dabbed the bottom of my eye with it. The speck adhered to it.

"Gotcha," she said.

She dried my tears with the Kleenex. She was very close and her scent swept over me. Neither of us moved.

Then she sat back, rolled the Kleenex into a ball, and threw it back into her purse.

I guess she'd made up her mind about me because she decided to open up regarding her family. "They're grifters."

"I'm sorry?"

"My brothers. My father, too. Basically they're small-time con artists who managed to hit it big. My brother, Barry, found a con for which he was ideally suited. He developed it, and with help from my father, expanded it."

"That's a pretty cynical thing to say."

"Not if you think his piety is phony." She turned to face me. "Are you married?"

"No. Are you?"

"No. Have you ever been married?"

"No. You?"

"No."

"So, what's with de Winter?"

"You mean my name?"

"Yes."

"An alias."

"Why?"

"I use it for my blog."

"Why de Winter?"

"Joan Fontaine."

"I beg your pardon?"

"The movie *Rebecca.* Joan Fontaine was Mrs. de Winter."

"Mrs. de Winter was a character in the movie?"

"She was. It's one of the better Hitchcock films. It's about lies and deception. Subjects not unfamiliar to me."

"And you adopted the name because…"

"It saves me from being identified as a member of the infamous Long family. Protects me from being constantly accosted by religious freaks."

"So it's not your married name."

"No."

"And you've never been married?"

"Just like you. Why not?"

I thought about that for several moments. "I can't really say. I never had the urge. You?"

"I never wanted to be tied down. To feel owned. Are you gay?"

"No. You?"

"No."

"Well, I'm glad we got that straightened out," I said.

She picked up a fallen pine cone and began pulling it apart. "She's a smart girl."

"Catharine?"

"Yes. She was onto them, and by the time Barry hit it big, a subtle distance had developed between them. She was conflicted. She was part of the act, but the act had grown to include their personal life. She had become a celebrity in her own right and, between you and me, she loved it. She gave birth to Three, who rounded out the pretty picture. The People's Pastor. The People's Pastor's beautiful family. What a joke. The thing is, they had suddenly become rock stars and found themselves stuck with each other."

"Do you know about the financial debacle?"

"Somewhat."

"How so?"

"I'm economically tethered to the nest, you see. I came here on their dime and they foot all of the bills."

"So?"

"One day it stopped. About three months ago. When I questioned my father about it, he told me the well had run dry."

"What about Hickey?"

"The space man? The un-favorite son? You ever try talking to Hickey? He's a total degenerate. I can't believe we emerged from the same womb. What about girlfriends?"

"What?"

"Are you seeing anyone?"

I started blinking rapidly. "I can barely see you."

"Very funny. Are you?"

"No. You?"

"No."

"What about your other brother?"

"The most Reverend Barry Clueless? He bought the whole ball of wax. His head is so far up his ass he can't see anything for the shit. What do you know about it?"

"I'm hearing they got burned by a Madoff-style Ponzi scheme. Barry, Senior, is bringing every pressure he can muster to prevent the news from breaking before next week's Celebration."

"Why?"

"If the faithful were to learn the Reverend's been taken, and for how much, he's afraid Barry the younger would topple off his golden pedestal. He wants to believe the hordes won't care, that they're totally in his thrall, but the old bastard has become one nervous guy."

"And Catharine?"

"My guess is she learned the truth and reacted to it. They either stashed her somewhere to keep her quiet or possibly even murdered her to ensure her silence.

"Jesus," she said. "I had no idea."

She stood and wandered out of the glen. I followed. When I reached her, she turned to me. I put my arms around her and she buried her face in my shoulder. After a while she leaned back and looked at me. "It's ironic, isn't it? Con men falling prey to other con men."

She moved closer, enough so that her mouth was nano-inches from mine. Her moist tongue darted out and slowly circled my lips, then pushed into my mouth. She exhaled a sweet, coffee-scented breath that ignited my senses. Her lips were remarkably soft and I kept on kissing them.

Then she stepped away and headed for the road. She stopped and turned to look at me. "This is crazy."

"Why?"

"Because I don't know you. I have no idea who you are. All I know is that you're a cop who's investigating my family. This could never work."

She spotted a fallen pine cone and kicked it soccer style into the woods. "There's also another reason."

"Which is?"

"I'm trouble."

"What kind of trouble?"

"It's complicated. I have responsibilities. Obligations. In an odd way, I'm spoken for."

"Which means?"

"Let's just say I'm unavailable and leave it at that."

• • ● • •

I headed back to Freedom with the taste of her still haunting me. I knew I was heading into weirdness. Every ounce of rationality I possessed was flashing warning signals to that effect. But she was in my head and I wanted her.

I hadn't had feelings like these since I can't remember when. I had nearly forgotten what obsession felt like and no matter how much I tried to convince myself otherwise, I knew that if I pursued her, trouble and uncertainty were sure to be in my future.

Maybe so, but for the first time in ages, I felt alive.

Chapter Twenty-eight

When I looked at the clock, it read six-thirty and the phone was ringing.

I answered it and found Johnny Kennerly on the other end. "What?"

"How long will it take you to get dressed and meet me in front of your building?"

"Why?"

"We have a triple homicide."

"What do you know?"

"Not much yet, but I'll know more by the time you climb your ass into my cruiser. Five minutes?"

"Ten."

• • ● • •

"This won't be pretty," Johnny said.

"Triples never are. What do we know about the victims?"

"Two men, one woman."

"ID?"

"Nothing official."

We were headed for the Freedom foothills, the most

exclusive neighborhood in the county, with our siren screaming.

"House belongs to a guy called Oliver Darien. Ever hear of him?"

"The financier?"

"Is that what he is?"

"I've heard a lot about him. Especially lately."

"How so?"

"He was about to be indicted."

"For?"

"Running a Ponzi scheme on a scale not dissimilar to Bernard Madoff's."

We turned into the circular driveway of the Darien estate, a Tudor-style mega-home, constructed in the 1920s on ten-plus acres. Pines and heritage oaks towered over the property which boasted an Olympic-sized pool, a tennis court with stadium seating for thirty, and a three-hole putting green.

Police barricades had already been erected in anticipation of a media frenzy. Crowds of gawkers were arriving, cluttering the street, clustering by the gate, many of them snapping photos and videos with cameras and cell phones.

We were met at the mansion's ornate porte cochere by Sheriff's Deputy Al Striar.

"It happened in the foyer," Striar said. "We've sealed it off. Be better if you entered through the back of the house."

"Who found it?"

"Housekeeper. When she showed up for work."

I frowned. "I'll need the house quarantined. No one in or out. Nothing disturbed. Please arrange for a CSI unit. The coroner, too."

"Got it." Striar reached for his cell phone.

Johnny and I circled the house on a gravel pathway bordered with hedgerows and flower beds. We entered through the kitchen, a monument to granite and polished cherrywood.

A local Freedom police officer guided us through an outsized living room that featured a collection of understuffed, uncomfortable-looking furniture, pale green walls, hand-designed moulding, and a muted yellow ceiling. We walked past a formal dining room that featured a mahogany table already set for twenty, and finally into the foyer, the scene of the crime.

Morning light filtered through a pair of narrow, stained-glass windows that bordered the front door. A carpeted grand staircase with filigreed banisters led to the upper floors.

Two bodies were sprawled out on the richly tiled floor. A third lay on the staircase. A fair amount of blood and tissue had been splattered everywhere.

Directly in front of the main entrance lay a man's body. He had been shot once in the head and had fallen backward, landing face-up on the black-and-white tile floor. He wore a blue terry cloth bathrobe and scuffed slippers.

Behind him was the body of another man who had also been shot in the head. He, too, had fallen backward and lay spread-eagled at the foot of the stairs.

Something about the body didn't appear right to me. I knelt beside the fallen man to have a look. His hands caught my attention. The thumb and index finger of his right hand were both out of joint and lay askew. As did the thumb of his left hand.

"That must have hurt," I mused.

I stepped carefully to the remains of a woman who lay sprawled across several steps of the grand staircase. She had been shot once in the chest. From the position of the body, it appeared as if she had collapsed and then slid headfirst down several steps.

Johnny Kennerly looked up from the blood trail left behind by the woman. "What do you make of it?"

"Looks like a surprise late night visit. Guy in the blue bathrobe opens the door and gets shot for his trouble. The other man is the intended target. Most likely he's Oliver Darien. Probably came downstairs to see who rang his doorbell in the middle of the night.

"From the look of it, I'd say the shooter makes him suffer a bit before dispatching him. Plays havoc with his hands. Thumbs wrenched out of their sockets. Fingers broken. Pretty nasty stuff.

"Woman is likely Mrs. Darien, who also came downstairs to check things out. Each of the victims knew the shooter."

Johnny looked away from the crime scene and turned to me. "How do you know?"

"Mr. Blue Bathrobe would never have opened the door to a stranger."

"What do we do now?"

I motioned to Johnny and turned toward the rear of the house. "We let the forensics techs do their jobs and we evaluate their discoveries. I suspect the Staties and the Feebs will want in on this one. It's bound to capture national media attention. Particularly if the Justice Department reveals its findings regarding Darien's

Ponzi scandal. Much too juicy a story to keep the big boys at bay."

"So?"

"So, we welcome them with open arms and abide the events. I want to hear what Norma Richard has to say."

"The coroner."

"I want to know what more she learns about the condition of Darien's body."

"What do you think?"

"Darien was tortured. He suffered a great deal of physical abuse."

"Any ideas as to who might have done it?"

"None I want to talk about."

"Because?"

"This is just the beginning."

Marsha Russo answered her cell phone on the first ring. "Speak to me."

I asked, "Where are you?"

"Off duty."

"Where off duty?"

"That would be none of your business."

"What if I were in need of you?"

"Are you?"

"Crime scene techs are crawling all over the Darien estate collecting DNA."

"And you want to know if any of it matches what's on the gloves."

"You sure know how to put two and two together."

"You think I can assist the process?"

"Nobody better than you."

"You know what they say about flattery?"

"No. What do they say?"

"Cute. Okay. I'll get on it."

"Thank you."

"The Shoe Barn."

"Excuse me?"

"I'm at The Shoe Barn."

"Because?"

"A girl can't have enough shoes."

"Hopefully this won't be an inconvenience for you."

"Sadly the Uggs will have to wait," she lamented and ended the call.

Chapter Twenty-nine

"What happened up there?"

We were in my father's office, a commanding room on the top floor of the County Courthouse, filled with heavy furniture and the souvenirs of a lengthy career.

Pictures and awards graced bookshelves and walls, most notable among them photos of my father with President Reagan, Clint Eastwood, and the two-time Governor of California, Jerry Brown.

Weakened, the Sheriff had settled into his ancient leather armchair.

"Nothing I can prove," I said.

"But something you believe."

"Yes."

"What?"

"The killer gained uncontested entry to the house. It was the live-in houseman who answered the door. The killer was known to him."

"Okay."

"This was going to be a big week for Oliver Darien. The Justice Department had concluded its investigation and the Feds were preparing to bust him, which would seriously impact a whole lot of people. Billy Goldman told me the Long family was doing everything they could to stall the Darien indictment until after the holy hoopla Celebration. Afraid that once the story broke, the press, and the celebrants watching on worldwide TV, would respond negatively, not only with regards to the size of the financial loss, but to the fact that sacred funds were heavily invested, as opposed to being used for the benefit of the flock, as intended."

"Meaning the well could run dry."

"It could."

"You believe the Longs were involved in the Darien murders."

"I do."

"Because?"

"Vengeance."

My father sat quietly for a while, deep in thought. Then he blurted, "Who?"

"It could have been anyone in their circle. One of the hired thugs, perhaps. Even Hickey himself."

"Why Hickey?"

"Coply intuition."

"But you have no proof," he said.

"Not yet."

"What do you want to do?"

"Leak it to the media."

"Leak the story of the Long family's connection to Oliver Darien?"

"Yes."

"Reveal their losses."

"Yes."

"Where?"

"Wherever it will do the most harm. I'm guessing CNN for openers."

"Why?"

"Following so hot on the heels of the Madoff debacle, the murder of Oliver Darien is likely to dominate the headlines. The story could conceivably overshadow the news regarding the identities of the scam victims."

"Which is why you want to release their names now?"

"Yes."

"Which would guarantee the story hitting before the revival Celebration."

"There's that."

"Which could do considerable damage to the Longs."

"We can only hope."

"And you want my blessing?"

"You're the Sheriff."

"Okay."

"Okay what?"

"Go for it."

Chapter Thirty

My cell phone had a bunch of messages on it, one from the coroner, Norma Richard.

"There's good news and bad news," Norma said when I reached her.

"What's the bad news?"

"Darien was pretty beaten up. You saw the hands. There was also significant bruising in the genital area."

"Suggesting?"

"Torture. Someone kicked him in the gonads. More than once and exceptionally hard."

"Ouch."

"Indeed."

"You think he was brutalized into divulging information?"

"I'm the coroner, Buddy. That's a detective question."

"Thanks, Norma."

"My pleasure."

"What's the good news?"

"I beg your pardon?"

"You said there was bad news and good news. What's the good news?"

"I'm planning on taking the rest of the day off."
"For?"
"Spiritual rejuvenation."
"Which means?"
"I'm headed for the mall."

Chapter Thirty-one

"There's bad news and even worse bad news," Marsha Russo announced when I entered the station.

I picked up my mail and started perusing it. "What's the first bad news?"

"There's no match."

I stopped looking at the mail. "I beg your pardon?"

"There's no DNA match for the gloves."

"They're certain?"

She nodded.

"What about on the bodies? Oliver Darien's, for example? Somebody beat him up pretty good."

Marsha picked up a sheet of paper from her desk and read aloud from it. "No DNA other than that of the victims themselves was discovered on the bodies."

I thought about that for several moments. "He was wearing gloves. Had to have been. His modus operandi. Remember the Rolex."

"So you think Hickey did it?"

"I know he did. I just can't prove it yet."

Marsha's face registered a moment of consternation.

"What's the rest of the bad news?" I asked.

"I couldn't prevent it."

"Prevent what?"

She pointed to my office. "You'll see."

With a sideways glance at her I stepped inside where I found Maggie de Winter sprawled out on my desk chair, feet up, staring out the window. She swiveled around to face me.

"This is a very good chair."

I looked at her.

"At least pretend you're happy to see me."

"I'm stunned is all."

"You don't strike me as a person who stuns easily."

She stood. She had on a transparent black vampire shirt, complete with a filigree lacework neckpiece worn over form-fitting black jazz pants. A pair of over-the-knee, bacon-colored Chinese Laundry boots completed her ensemble.

"You sure know how to make a girl feel all fuzzy and wanted."

She walked to the door and closed it. Then she came over and put her arms around my neck.

"I've never done it in a Sheriff's office."

"And you're not going to start now."

"I knew you'd say that."

She kissed me and despite myself, I kissed her back. She looked at her watch. "Do you live nearby?"

"It's a small town."

"If I left now, how long would it take me to get to your place?"

"Five minutes. Eight tops."

"You're sure about not doing it here."

I nodded.

"What's the address?"

I wrote it down.

"I'll meet you there," she proposed.

"You mean now?"

"You have something better to do?"

She pulled her car keys from her pocket and dangled them in front of me. She pointed to her watch and winked at me.

"Eight minutes," she teased and left the office.

Marsha Russo appeared in my doorway. "Who's the babe?"

"Don't ask."

"I already know, just in case you take me for a total moron. You realize you're making a huge mistake."

"You think?"

"You stand a very good chance of her doing considerable damage to your reputation, both personally and professionally."

"I do."

"You know this."

I nodded.

"And you don't care."

"I didn't say that."

"So what are you going to do about it?"

"I'm going to damn well put a stop to it."

"Liar."

"Why would you say that?"

"Because of the look in your eye."

"What look?"

"Male pattern stupidity."

Chapter Thirty-two

In hindsight, I believe it happened because I was distracted and less diligent than I might otherwise have been.

I paid little attention to the Harley lowrider that moved swiftly along the second floor of the County Courthouse parking structure where my Wrangler was parked.

I had yanked the door open when I spotted two riders dressed in black, both wearing dual visors and full face helmets, the rider in back holding a .357 Magnum revolver.

I almost managed to duck out of the way when he fired, but the hollow point bullet slammed into my left shoulder as I dived for cover. The assailants kept going.

I was able to wrest the cell phone from my pocket and call Wilma, but, although help arrived within minutes, the Harley had vanished.

Johnny Kennerly was the first to show up, having run to the parking structure directly from the office. He had barely begun to examine my bloody wound when the medics arrived and took over. They did their best to stanch the bleeding. They loaded me into the ambulance for the five-minute drive to Freedom Adventist Hospital, where I was rushed to the emergency room and moments later, into surgery.

The bullet narrowly missed an artery and lodged in my shoulder. It did a fair amount of tissue damage, which the surgical team was able to repair once they removed the bullet.

"You were lucky," Dr. Alan Klein said when he paid his postsurgical visit. "If we hadn't gotten to you when we did, you'd likely have bled out."

I'm sure I said something clever but I was too sedated to remember. I awakened later to find Marsha Russo sleeping upright in the chair beside my bed, an open book on her lap, her hennaed red hair a mess.

I was attached to several drips and my shoulder was bandaged. I must have been on painkillers because it felt as if songbirds had nested in my brain. I struggled to remember what happened and to identify where I was.

Marsha sensed I was awake because her eyes fluttered opened and she stared at me for awhile. Then, in a voice husky with sleep, she whispered, "Say something."

"Is that you, Bob?"

"Very funny. Do you remember anything that happened?

"From the look of things, I'd say I was shot."

"You were. Do you know who did it?"

"He was wearing a helmet."

"Why?"

Despite being weak-voiced and dopey, I couldn't resist joking. "Because it's required by law."

I was aware of Marsha shaking her head. When I opened my eyes again, my father was sitting in the chair. "What's up?" I said.

"You are. How do you feel?"

"Lousy. What are you doing here?"

"Worrying."

"I'm sorry, Dad. This must be awful for you. Go home."

"You'll be pleased to know the doctors say you're in no danger."

"All the more reason for you to go home."

When I opened my eyes again, Johnny Kennerly was in the chair. "What day is it?"

"It's still Thursday."

"Why am I so gaga?"

"Morphine."

"Why?"

"They don't want you suddenly leaping out of bed and trying to find the guy who shot you."

"I'm not likely to do that."

"They want to make certain."

"Stop them."

"Stop who?"

"The idiots who are keeping me sedated."

"I'll look into it."

When I awakened again, I was less batty and attached to only one drip. Sunshine streamed through the window. No one was sitting in the chair. There was a call button attached to the bed sheet and I pressed it.

Within moments, a severe-looking older woman in a nurse's uniform appeared, holding a small plastic cup of apple juice.

"Well, looky here," she said. "He's awake."

She removed the straw that was attached to the cup, punched it through the hole on top and placed it on the over-bed table in front of me.

"Fluids," she admonished. "Fluids are the key. Fluids lead to solids which in turn lead to getting out of here. You want my advice, drink fluids. Lots of fluids."

She headed for the door. "I'll let the doctor know you're awake," she said. "And taking the fluids."

Chapter Thirty-three

I was released on the morning of my second day, accompanied by a private-duty nurse and a police escort. They helped me into my own bed. I was heavily bandaged and my left arm was in a sling.

I felt better although uncomfortable and in no small amount of pain. I tried my best not to down any of the little blue pills that sat next to the water carafe on my nightstand, but I wasn't always successful.

Among the debris accumulated in my mailbox was a handwritten note from Maggie de Winter, postmarked Los Angeles.

"I waited," she wrote. "You never showed. Probably for the best. You know where to find me."

She hadn't signed it.

I assumed the story didn't have legs enough to appear in the L.A. media, so she likely had no idea what happened to me.

I drifted in and out of consciousness in a blue pill haze. I dreamed I had been set up. My misanthropic self insinuated it was no coincidence that Maggie and the shooter showed up at the same time. My idealistic self waved me off. I slept fitfully.

In addition to a supply of non-genetically modified Whole Foods snacks and meals, Johnny Kennerly had also brought the morning papers.

The Darien murder was front page news in the *L.A. Times*, and according to Johnny, had been picked up by CNN, MSNBC, Fox News, and the four networks. The national dailies, also.

The story went viral on the Internet. *The Huffington Post* website reported that, according to reliable sources, Oliver Darien was to have been indicted on the very day he was murdered.

His victims, investors everywhere on the planet, expressed shock and outrage. The Attorney General promised a thorough investigation. FBI agents swarmed Darien's offices.

In a flurry of late-breaking news, CNN reported exclusively that numbered among Darien's victims were the Reverend Barry Long, Junior, and The Heart of Our Saviour Ministry.

The talk shows were soon overbooked with suppliers telling tales of having been shortchanged or stiffed entirely by the Longs, of providing the Ministry with significant credit lines, which resulted in failed businesses and incipient bankruptcies.

Efforts to reach Reverend Barry Long, Junior, or his father, had thus far proved fruitless.

My thoughts constantly tracked back to the shooting. Although my memory was faulty, something about it stuck in my mind.

The vision of the motorcycle bearing down on me kept playing over and over in my head. Something was familiar about the driver but I couldn't quite place what it was. Just when I hit the threshold of figuring it out, it faded.

Lying around the house didn't agree with me. In no time I was out of bed and feeling claustrophobic. Cranky, too. When Johnny offered to drive me to the office, I accepted.

The nurse helped dress and load me into a cruiser. Once at the station, I was greeted warmly and everyone did their best to make me feel welcome and loved.

I was sitting at my desk, surrounded by a coterie of deputies, all clambering to tell me what they had been up to in my absence.

When it was Al Striar's turn, he mentioned the research he had done at my request regarding Milton Pfenster. As soon as he spoke the name, I knew it was him.

Milton Pfenster was the driver of the Harley.

Chapter Thirty-four

We maneuvered the winding driveway to the Long family manse and when we reached the parking level we were once again greeted by Jeffrey Bruce.

As I stepped out of the cruiser, assisted by Johnny Kennerly, Jeffrey stared at my arm which was wrapped in a sling. "What happened?"

"I fell."

He looked at me dubiously. "Okay. What can we do for you this time?"

"I'd like to speak with Milton Pfenster."

"I'm afraid Milton is no longer with us."

"No longer with you?"

"That's right. He left."

"You mean he quit his job?"

"I'm not certain he quit, but one way or the other, he's gone."

"He's moved off of the property?"

"He has."

"When?"

"I think it was last Tuesday. Yes. It was definitely last Tuesday."

The day of the Darien killings. Johnny and I exchanged a glance. "May I see his dwelling?"

"Excuse me?"

"I'd like to have a look at the place where he was living."

Jeffrey retreated into his thoughts for several moments. "I'm not sure I can permit that."

"Jeffrey?"

"Yes?"

"Remember the last time I was here?"

"Who could forget?"

"Exactly. Would you like a repeat performance?"

"Do you have a warrant?"

"Let me put it this way. I could have one within hours, but I'd feel a whole lot less kindly toward you if I was forced to go through that exercise again."

"What would I tell the Reverend?"

"What I just told you."

He didn't say anything.

"Jeffrey?"

"Yes?"

"Would you please show us Milton's place?"

After several moments, he said, "Follow me."

• • ● • •

The cabin Milton Pfenster lived in was little more than a shack. It consisted of a single living area plus a half-kitchen and a tiny bathroom. It appeared undisturbed since Milton's departure. A fair amount of debris littered the hardwood floor. A few items of clothing had been left behind. Assorted magazines and newspapers lay scattered on the room's only table and on a tattered armchair.

Johnny and I poked around but found nothing of note. We stepped outside. The cabin was situated in the woods, surrounded by pine and oak trees, as well as a plethora of indigenous greenery.

I circled the perimeter of the small structure and had I not nearly stumbled on it, I would never have seen the manhole cover that lay nearly invisible amid the tall grass and fallen leaves.

I called out to Johnny, who joined me. "What do you make of this?"

I kicked leaves and grass aside and pointed to the cover.

"Sewer line?"

"Not likely. I'm thinking the property would have wells and some kind of septic system."

"Why the manhole, then?"

"Good question."

"What say we find out."

The grounds around Milton Pfenster's cabin were as unkempt as the cabin itself. No landscaping attention had been paid in ages. Buffalo and Bermuda grasses grew wild and tall. Agaves, fuchsia, and desert mallows fought for space with monkeyflowers, sage, and California poppies. Horticultural chaos reigned.

Johnny went in search of something to remove the manhole cover. "There has to be some kind of device around here for prying it open," he mused.

He began a slow turn around the outside of the cabin. He was on the other side of the structure when I heard him cry out, "Eureka."

"Gold?"

"Better."

He appeared brandishing a slender steel rod with a forked end.

By inserting the end into a pair of corresponding slits in the manhole cover, he raised it and slid it off. We looked inside and discovered a concrete-lined pit, wide enough for a man to traverse, with a metal ladder bolted to the wall. Johnny found a light switch near the top of the ladder. When he flipped it on, wall sconces illuminated the pit.

We stared at each other, considering. Inasmuch as my shoulder was still in a sling, I motioned for Johnny to do the exploring.

He climbed down the ladder. When he reached the bottom, he yelled up to me. "Holy shit!"

"What?"

"There's a tunnel down here."

"Tell me."

"It's fully lighted and paved. From the look of it, I'm guessing it leads to the house."

• • ● ● •

I was standing with Jeffrey Bruce in the basement of the mansion, in the room containing the three cells, when a section of wall suddenly slid backward and Johnny Kennerly climbed through the opening. "Well, I'll be damned," I said.

A look of astonishment appeared on Jeffrey's face. "Obviously you didn't know about this," I said to him.

"I had no idea any of this existed."

"You mean the cells?"

"And the tunnel. I hope this will help you solve the mystery. Disappearing like she did is a worry."

"Because?"

"People don't just vanish. Especially when they're her. She's a good person. I'm scared for her."

His comments were personal and heartfelt. It gave rise to some thought as to the nature of his relationship with Catharine. "I'm going to go out on a limb and surmise she's okay," I reassured him. "I'm also going to speculate the Longs built the tunnel. Most likely the cells, too."

"Why, do you suppose?" Johnny frowned.

"Good question. What's it like?"

"The tunnel? It's high and wide. And there's a storage area about halfway through."

"For what?"

"You mean what would they store there?"

"Yes."

"Just about anything, I guess."

I turned to Jeffrey.

"There's a back gate to the estate, yes?"

"Yes."

"Tunnel like this would keep certain comings and goings confidential."

I turned back to Johnny. "How fast can you get a forensics team out here?"

"As soon as I have authorization."

"You have it."

"I need it signed by Sheriff Steel."

"I'll have it faxed within the hour."

Johnny nodded.

I turned to Jeffrey Bruce. "What was his ride?"

"Excuse me?"

"Milton Pfenster. What did he drive?"

"Some kind of Harley. Souped up, too."

"You said you were an intern?"

"I did."

"If I'm not mistaken, interns don't get paid, correct?"

"There are other things besides money."

"Meaning?"

"I was a student at the Valley School of Film and Television, which proved to be disappointing. My internship with the Longs has provided me with a great deal of hands-on experience. I've learned more here about the way the real world works than I ever did at Valley."

"I'm sure that's a benefit, but things being what they are here now, you might want to set your sights elsewhere."

"I already have."

Chapter Thirty-five

I sent Marsha Russo and P.J. Lincoln to the Pavilion in search of Milton Pfenster and Hickham Long, both of whom I wanted brought in for questioning.

She phoned me from her cruiser. "They're gone."

"Both of them?"

"Yes."

"Did you find out where?"

"Hickey's alleged to be somewhere in South America. Security officer says he's the liaison between the Long family ministry and their TV partners south of the border."

"Pfenster?"

"No one seems to know where he is."

"Curiouser and curiouser." I replaced the receiver and was just settling in for some serious mulling when the intercom buzzed.

"Murray Kornbluth on four," Wilma said.

"What does he want?"

"Press the button below the flashing light to find out."

"Buddy Steel," I said, having done as I was instructed.

"One moment for Mr. Kornbluth," a nasal female voice said.

Within seconds, Kornbluth's booming voice rang out. "You should have stayed in L.A."

"Have you any other words of encouragement this morning, Murray?"

"What is it with you, Buddy? Every time I look up, I hear your name."

"So, don't look up."

"Always the wise ass. Before my blood begins to boil, tell me about Burton."

"It's not good, Murray."

"I heard Gehrig's."

"You heard right."

"Is there anything I can do?"

"Call him. Kibbitz him up. Irritate him like only you can."

"Will do," he said. "I'm sorry about this, Buddy."

"Thanks, Murray."

After a brief silence, Kornbluth went on. "What is it with you and the Longs?"

"Meaning?"

"Why are you dogging them? What's between you and Hickey?"

"Well, for starters, somebody shot me."

"Listen, Buddy. You're totally misguided if you think it was Hickey who shot you. Besides, he was out of the country."

"He was out of the country four days ago?"

"Read my lips, Buddy. He didn't do it."

"Where's Catharine?"

"Resting."

"Resting where?"

"None of your business."

"Of course it's my business. First I get a reliable report that Catharine's gone missing and may have been murdered. Then I hear the Longs are bouncing checks all over town. Barry, Senior, turns out to be a prime victim of Oliver Darien's Ponzi scam and then Darien turns up dead. I also have reason to believe that the missing Milton Pfenster was driving the motorbike that carried the gunman who shot me."

"May I respond to this ludicrousness?"

"Have I a choice?"

"It's all bullshit, Buddy. Forget Catharine. She's alive and well. She suffered a little psychological meltdown and she's currently recuperating in a credible facility. It's true that the Longs have had some financial reversals, but they're on the rebound and fully intend to honor their commitments. As for the implication that any member of the Long family shot anyone…you, Oliver Darien, or the tooth fairy, for that matter…you carry forward with that line of inquiry and you're going to buy yourself a career-ending lawsuit."

"Oh, my God. I'm shaking like a leaf."

"I'm not kidding, Buddy."

"Hickey did it. And he knows I know he did."

"Don't say I didn't warn you."

He slammed the phone in my ear.

Chapter Thirty-six

We agreed to meet at The Malibu Inn, a small, luxury hotel located on the beach in the heart of the legendary Colony.

I had been cleared to drive and made the trip down the scenic Pacific Coast Highway in well under two hours. The manager upgraded me to an ocean view suite where I was now resting on the terrace, on one of the two lounge chairs, a gin and tonic sweating on the table beside me.

Maggie let herself in, gazed around the suite, dropped her overnight bag and joined me outside. "Isn't this swell," she commented.

We both stared at the gently rolling Pacific and at Catalina Island in the distance. She sat next to me on the lounge chair, then leaned over and kissed me.

"Mmm," she said. "Gin."

She was wearing a low-cut, lightweight sheath dress that provided a terrific view of her amazing body. She was about to climb on top of me when I winced.

A look of concern appeared on her face. "What?"

"Nothing."

"Come on. What is it?"

I told her.

"My God. That's why you never showed up?"

"That and a battery of post-surgery narcotics."

As I watched her consider this news, I was still wary about the possibility that she could have set me up. Her ardor was unaffected. "We'll need to be very cautious."

She stood and shrugged out of her dress. She wore only a thong. She reached for my hand and when I gave it to her, she placed it between her legs.

"I'd bet anything there's a bed around here somewhere."

"Would you like me to help you find it?"

"I would. And quickly, too."

We spent the twilight hours wrapped around each other, paying little attention to the setting sun or the diminishing light.

We connected deeply and enjoyed the myriad plateaux we reached both separately and together. She was agile and learned, and after taking note of my damaged shoulder, she was also tender yet at the same time thrilling. It was all pretty good and I let go of my trepidation and surrendered to it.

At last she got up and wandered about the suite, turning on a few lights. She stretched and yawned.

"Were you planning to feed me?"

"Only if it proved necessary."

"It's necessary."

"There's a pretty nice restaurant downstairs."

"Last one there is a monkey's uncle."

The stark wooden interior of the Malibu Inn bistro was softened by candlelight and muted music. It held just twelve tables, most of them empty. The waitstaff slipped unobtrusively through the room, anticipating and serving.

Sated both sexually and now gastronomically, we sat sipping the last of our Prosecco beneath a canopy of glistening stars.

She placed her empty glass on the table. "We've certainly managed to avoid talking about the elephant in the room."

"Meaning?"

"Whatever in the hell it is that's going on with you and my family."

"I thought you had distanced yourself from them."

"You can only distance yourself so far when you're tethered financially."

"So you're in touch with them."

"Only with my father. He wants to know why you're dogging them."

"Where else have I heard that same expression?"

She didn't respond, which helped raise my suspicions. "You've spoken with Murray Kornbluth."

"He is the family solicitor."

"Why do I have the feeling we're suddenly treading on thin ice here?"

"Why do you?"

"Because I'm conducting an investigation that involves them."

"Which Murray claims is groundless."

"I knew this was a mistake."

A pair of newcomers entered the restaurant and were seated next to us at a window table.

Maggie ignored them. "I told you I was trouble."

"I didn't realize it was that kind of trouble."

"What do you want to do?"

"I don't know, Maggie. I'm more than slightly nuts about you. What we just did only heightens those feelings."

"And you think I don't share them?"

"I didn't say that."

"What exactly did you say?"

"I may have misled myself. It wouldn't be the first time. I somehow thought you existed in a universe separate from them. Now I see I was wrong."

"Why would it matter?"

"Ethics."

"Don't go all ethics on me, Buddy. I told you things with me are complicated. I said I had obligations. Now you're on your high horse looking down at me and talking ethics. You think this was a mistake? Well, so do I."

She flashed me a look of exasperation, stood and sighed theatrically. "Give me five minutes."

"For what?"

"To collect my things."

She stepped over to me, knelt down, and kissed me. "At least we'll always have Paris."

She looked at me for a moment, then left.

I sat alone.

I paid the bill and checked out of the inn.

I got home at around two and knocked back enough gin to allow me to put her out of my mind for a while.

Chapter Thirty-seven

"State Police located Milton Pfenster," Marsha Russo said when I arrived at the office.

"Where?"

"Hikers found him in a ditch in a section of forest just south of Big Sur."

"Living?"

"Not anymore."

"How?"

"Initial reports suggest a motorcycle accident. Body was in tatters, victim of some kind of wild animal attack. Not a whole lot left of him."

"Charming."

"You think he was murdered?"

"I do."

"Because?"

"He knew too much."

"What now?"

"I need to talk with the Sheriff."

It wasn't a good day for the Sheriff. He was having

difficulty with his speech. His slurred words couldn't keep up with the pace of his thoughts.

We were in the den, where he was swaddled in a blanket and seated on his favorite chair in front of a fire that needed more wood. "Would you put a couple logs on the fire for me, Buddy?"

"Sure thing."

Using a pair of metal tongs, I hoisted two quartered sections of pine logs from the stack beside the stone fireplace, and placed them on top of the smoldering fire. It wasn't long before they burst into flame.

"That's good," he said. "Thank you."

I sat back down and we stared silently at the fire for a while.

"So, what would you do?" I finally asked.

"It's a tough call. So much speculation. Such a sensitive time."

"Because of the Celebration?"

"Because of everything. To my surprise, I'm being told there's a fair amount of sympathetic concern for the Reverend. It's likely he'll throw himself on people's mercy and his flock will be more than inclined to cut him some slack."

"Because?"

"He's young. He's got a family. There's a case to be made that his involvement was peripheral. His stated purpose is to bring God to those who need Him most. He'll likely argue that the money-changers never figured in his thinking."

"And you believe that?"

"What I believe is irrelevant," my father said. "I also suspect that Murray Kornbluth has a surprise lurking up his sleeve."

"Such as?"

"Such as producing Catharine at the most opportune moment."

"The opening session."

"That certainly qualifies as an opportune moment."

"And Barry, Senior?"

"It might take some time, but unless you can prove he was directly involved in the murders, he stands a pretty good chance of skating."

"He masterminded it. Milton Pfenster and Hickey carried it out."

"How do you know?"

"I know. Revenge is a qualifiable motive. The Long family never planned on being broke again. Money was their ticket to respectability and position. The size of their loss will catch people's attention, and the fact that the money wasn't being applied where it was supposed to be applied will more than likely draw critical scrutiny by the media."

"So?" my father said.

"There's something else. Something I can't quite put my finger on. I can smell it but I can't see it. I need some help."

"From me?"

"Yes, from you. The size of the Long family losses has yet to be revealed. I want to know how much they lost. And more importantly, I want to know how those losses reconcile with the income they declared with the IRS."

"Because?"

"If I'm right, it won't add up."

"Was there anything else?"

"I need access to Oliver Darien's datebook. I want to know who he met with and how frequently over the last weeks of his life."

"Feds control those records now."

"But you can access them."

"Why do you say that?"

"Because you know all the big fish."

"Why would you think the big fish would tell me anything?"

"Because you're Burton Steel. That's why."

Chapter Thirty-eight

When you're born and grow up in a small town, everyone knows you. They know all about you. Their opinions of you are formed early in your life and are damned near impossible to change.

I was my father's son. I was dutifully at his side whenever the occasion called for it. We were anything but close, but were frequently together.

Johnny Kennerly was his protégé. He and I were aware of each other from an early age, but kept our distance. Although we both grew up in Freedom, it was on opposite sides of the tracks. We went to different schools and our circle of friends was dissimilar. So it was a surprise when he pulled me aside and told me that someone we had both known from the past wanted to set up a meeting with us.

Feliciano "Chanho" Pineda had also grown up in Freedom. He was the son of El Salvadoran immigrants who worked hard to make a good life for their family. As a kid, Chanho had been gang-affiliated, but he became an athlete of some repute. Johnny and I knew him because we were all gym rats and had made each other's acquaintance on various basketball courts throughout the county.

Although Chanho left the gang when he was accepted at Cal Poly, he remained close to many of his gangland associates, and over time, played an important role in helping rehabilitate a number of them and assist in their efforts to achieve legitimacy. He was a member of the Mayor's Community Relations Task Force and was greatly admired in the neighborhood.

He was jumbo-sized, having added weight once his playing days were over. A flattened nose, the victim of any number of beneath-the-boards encounters with meaty hands and flying elbows, haphazardly adorned the center of his large face. His restless brown eyes were guarded, his manner wary.

I joined him and Johnny at Lesnick's coffee shop. They were drinking shakes. I settled for black coffee.

"Looking good, Chanho." We briefly hugged. "It's been too long."

"You still got game?"

"In my dreams. Regardless of what anyone tells you, it *is* the legs that go first."

"Tell me about it."

"Chanho has some information he believes might be of interest," Johnny said.

"I'm all ears."

"There's some heavy shit going down in the community," Chanho said.

"Okay."

"I'm telling you this in confidence. We're clear on that, right?"

"Yes."

"You know I used to be a member of the Blackbirds."

"I do."

"Do you know the Blackbirds have developed a working relationship with a faction of the Sinaloan cartel?"

"I've heard the rumors."

"Well, there's a tangle. It seems the Birds are owed a significant amount of money by one of their associates. A local guy."

"For?"

"An investment they made with him."

"What kind of investment?"

"The local guy had been financing some drug-related activities for the Birds."

"Such as?"

"This and that. It's not really relevant."

"Okay."

"They trusted him. They made some dough together. So when he offered the brothers a chance to be a part of what he described as a non-risk, short-term financial bonanza, they went along with him. Some of the money they invested belonged to the Sinaloans."

"And the Sinaloans sanctioned the investment?"

"That's the tangle. They knew nothing about it."

"You mean the Birds invested cartel money without their knowledge."

"Yes."

"I'm guessing that was a mistake," I said.

"Big mistake," Chanho said. "The local guy disappeared. So did the money."

"And?"

"The Birds were forced to inform the cartel they couldn't pay them on time. The cartel doesn't value nonpayment. The blood between them and the Birds started running bad."

"Is there a punch line to this anecdote?"

"I was relating this story to Johnny and when I mentioned the local guy's name, he lit up."

"Hickham Long," I interjected softly.

Chanho glared at Johnny. "You told him?"

"Johnny never said a word."

Chanho turned back to me. "How did you know?"

"Figures. It's on the street that the Longs got taken for a bundle. They owe everyone."

"That's what we're just now learning. The Sinaloans are livid. They're demanding their money. They're threatening retribution. They red-flagged this Long guy. Their *soldados* are out hunting for him. Now they're dropping hints that they might even take out a few members of Hickey's family, one by one, until they cough up the dough."

"Taking out, as in…?"

"Ceasing them."

I considered this for a few moments. Then I queried, "The cartel thinks the Long family still has money?"

"Seems their accountant reached out to the Birds. He asked them to ease up for a few days. Said Hickey's got a bead on enough money to make them whole."

"Who's the accountant?"

"Guy named Bob Albanis."

"And this Albanis character claims the debt to the Birds will be repaid?"

"That's what he's saying."

"When?

"Soon."

"And they believe him?"

"They don't have a whole lot of options."

"You're in touch with them?"

"Yes."

"You're advising them?"

"I'm consulting with them."

"And?"

"I don't know, Buddy. I'm doing all I can to help avoid a gang war."

"I appreciate you telling me this, Chanho. It is alarming. Gang warfare is bad business. Raises everyone's temperature. I know you carry large mojo. I trust you can help defuse things."

"I'm doing what I can. No guarantees."

"I understand," I said. "How about we keep each other informed?"

He nodded and stood. "Johnny knows how to reach me."

He stared at us both for a moment, then slipped out of the coffee shop.

"What do you make of it?" Johnny said.

"It's tricky."

"Why do you think he told you about it?"

"So he could inform the Birds that I know what's going on," I answered.

"Why would he do that?"

"My guess is the Birds want to make certain the Sinaloans understand there will be consequences for any acts of violence. If they're made aware of the fact that local law enforcement knows what's going on and is prepared to intervene, perhaps they'll be less likely to act impulsively."

"You think Hickey will show with the money?"

"Yes."

"Because?"

"Not for the reasons they think."

"Why, then?"

"Because the dutiful son wants the heat taken off his old man."

"You think that's why he ex-ed Oliver Darien," Johnny said.

"He's fishing."

"For?"

"Anything Darien may have stashed."

"So, you think there's a stash?"

"I don't know how big, but I'd bet there's something."

Neither of us spoke for a while.

"One way or the other, I wouldn't give a plugged nickel for Hickham Long's chances of survival," I said.

"The cartel?"

"The Birds. Once he shows up here, if he shows up, he's toast. They'll deliver his head to the cartel on a platter."

"He shows up here, he's likely to have a rather large jones on for you. You haven't made his family's life any kind of picnic. He may well want your head on a platter."

"Life's a bitch, isn't it," I said.

"You need to take this more seriously, Buddy."

"I do, don't I?"

Chapter Thirty-nine

Her Honor the Mayor phoned in the early afternoon. "He's in Freedom General."

"Why?"

"He was having trouble breathing and it scared him. The doctor admitted him for observation. They put him on oxygen and he's feeling better."

"I'm on my way."

"Buddy…"

"Yes."

"Don't upset him." With that she hung up.

"Don't upset him." She just can't let it go. She has to keep jabbing the needle.

I was born in Freedom to near-normal parents. My father, who had yet to become Sheriff, was making his way as a local law enforcement officer and my mother was a stay-at-home mom who took loving care of my sister and me. We were a family.

All that changed when she got sick. Cancer. She didn't smoke or drink. She lived a healthy lifestyle. She was the least likely candidate.

It revealed itself as a lump in her breast. At first she ignored it. Cancer detection then wasn't the obsessive issue it is today. It was my father who insisted she visit the family physician. In short order, she was diagnosed, mastectomied, radiated, and the recipient of the news that she had metastasized into a stage four. She was gone in a matter of months.

Bereft and seeking something that would take his mind off of his anguish, my father buried himself in his work. Soon he began to explore the possibility of running for elected office. When the then-Sheriff chose to step down, Dad petitioned the County Board of Supervisors for their support in his bid for the office.

With his unrelenting energy and larger than life charisma, he was a shoo-in with the supervisors. Given their backing, he won the election handily.

It was when he took up offices in the County Court-house that he met Regina Goodnow. She was serving as chief of staff for then-Mayor Edward Rissien, whose headquarters were housed in the same building. Their paths crossed randomly, in the corridors, in the parking lot, in the cafeteria, but soon, they started crossing by design.

Both had lost spouses to illness and both were wounded and lonely. They married less than a year after my mother's death. The Sheriff and the Deputy Mayor. In a matter of months, I went from being a town nobody to the son of Freedom's most prominent couple.

My newly found status arrived before I had come to grips emotionally with the loss of my mother. I had become withdrawn and reclusive. My stepmother and

I didn't see eye to eye on things. She grew to dislike me. And I her.

She doted on her twin sons, Dan and Don, who were three years older than me. I didn't much care for them. They looked alike. They dressed alike. They were a pair of mindless, boring nitwits. I referred to them as Tweedle Dan and Tweedle Don. They never tired of teasing me.

It was when they were in tenth grade and I was in seventh that things changed. I had grown into my frame and over the course of a single summer, I gained twenty pounds and became bigger and stronger.

The twins were what I considered to be soft boys, fleshy and inert. When they were larger and weightier than I, they took great pleasure in making my life miserable. When I filled out, it somehow escaped their notice.

One memorable fall afternoon they were following me home from school, keeping a distance between us, but close enough to toss stones at me and giggle riotously as they did so. I asked them to stop but that only egged them on.

Finally, after they had managed to toss a handful of pebbles down the back of my shirt, I'd had enough. I singled out Tweedle Dan and punched him in the stomach, causing him to drop to his knees and hurl whatever remained of his lunch.

Tweedle Don ran away and I chased him. He wasn't very fit and the run taxed him. He collapsed in the front hallway of our house and passed out.

The housekeeper, finding Tweedle Don lying on the floor, began screaming that he was dead. She called the then Deputy Mayor and proceeded to inform her of that fact. Then she sat down on the kitchen floor and wept, moaning that Tweedle Don's death would surely cost her her job.

She was still wailing when Her Honor arrived to find Tweedle Don alive, both he and his brother in their room on their beds, playing video games.

Angry that her afternoon had been so egregiously interrupted, she fulfilled the housekeeper's prophesy by firing her on the spot. She went out of her way to find me and to wordlessly indict me with an angry glower. Then she went back to work.

Although they never physically accosted me again, the twins made it their business to poison the well for me with their mother whenever possible. There was always tension between Her Honor and me. She got along well enough with my sister, Sandra. But as for me, we shared a testy detente that continues to this day.

"Don't upset him."

She couldn't resist.

Chapter Forty

When I entered his room at Freedom General, my father removed the mask that was covering his nose and mouth and smiled weakly at me. The mask was attached to a noninvasive respirator that served to assist his breathing.

"I'm sorry, Buddy," he said. "I didn't mean to make everyone crazy. When I had trouble breathing, I panicked. I thought I was going to choke to death. I didn't mean to upset anyone."

"It's okay, Dad. I'm happy you're all right."

"It sucks, you know."

"I know."

"I've never been sick a day in my life. I can't for the life of me figure out how this happened."

"I understand."

"Not being able to breathe is brutal."

"At least you're all right now."

"For the moment."

He lay back, exhausted. We sat silently for a while. The hospital reeked of disinfectant. It had started to rain, and the sounds of heavy drops hitting the window, along with the low grade mechanical groaning of the non-invasive ventilator, seemed deafening.

The nurse's station was just across the hall, and through the open door I could make out the comings and goings of the world of medical professionals, serious, determined, and focused.

My father looked at me. "You were right."

"About?"

"The Longs. There's a discrepancy between their declared income and the size of their loss."

"Go on."

"I'm not supposed to have this information."

"Okay."

"It was given to me in confidence."

"Okay."

"Their declared net earnings for 2014 totaled somewhere in the neighborhood of eleven million. The amount of their losses with The Darien Group exceeded seventy."

"Seventy million dollars?"

"According to Darien's records."

"How could they have amassed that large a fortune in so short a time?"

"Pretty amazing."

"Pretty impossible, I'd say. Do the math. The Ministry was founded in 2008. They didn't even go on the air until 2010. Admittedly they captured people's attention and became an overnight phenomenon, but you don't clear that kind of dough that fast. Even if Oliver Darien inflated the value of their investments as part of his Ponzi scheme, it would have been impossible for them to have leapt that high."

"Could they have just blindly swallowed his line?"

"The Longs are con men. They couldn't be that gullible. They would have smelled a rat if their declared earnings with Darien were so inflated as to appear questionable."

"Maybe they were too greedy to notice. Just like the other victims. Like the Madoff crowd."

"There's another explanation."

"Go on."

"What if they were laundering drug money?"

"What makes you say that?"

"Hickey's run afoul of the Blackbirds. He owes them big time. They're looking for him and they're threatening retribution."

"How do you know?"

"Don't ask. The Longs saw a golden opportunity with Oliver Darien. Clearly Darien didn't care where the money invested with him came from. Although nobody knew it at the time, he was using it to finance his scam. He was as happy as a pig in shit when the Longs slipped more money into the pot because he knew it was going to further fuel his perfidy.

"And conversely, I submit the Longs believed they were pulling one over on him. They came to believe they could use the Darien Fund as a way to launder their drug money and at the same time, earn huge profits on it. They deluded themselves when they received Darien's phony statements. All they saw were dollar signs that kept growing larger."

"Except for the fact they weren't," my father said.

"When the Madoff scandal erupted, somebody commented, '*If it looks too good to be true, it most likely is.*'"

"Darien convinced himself he could remain unde-tected endlessly. Certainly the Longs had no idea what was going on. They placed everything they had with him."

"And neither the Longs or Darien ever saw disaster lurking."

"Not until it bit them in the ass."

My father laughed, which quickly turned into a coughing fit. When the spasms eased, he lay back on the pillow and closed his eyes. After several moments, he felt well enough to sit up and comment, "The pits."

"Maybe you should try and get some rest, Dad. I wouldn't want to wear you out."

Undeterred, he glared at me. "Don't think for one minute I'm worn out. I'm fine. Okay?"

He held his stare for several more moments, then offered, "I had a look at Darien's calendar."

"And?"

"It was as you suspected. He met with Hickey Long both on the day before and on the day he died."

"And on the night he died, too, no doubt."

"You think it was Hickey who tortured and killed him?"

"Hickey was desperate. I think he believed that despite Darien's financial collapse, he still had a stash hidden somewhere. Hickey tortured him in an effort to learn where it was and how he could access it."

"You think Darien told him?"

"I don't believe Darien could have withstood torture for very long. If there was a stash, I think he gave it up fairly quickly, believing that by so doing, he'd save his life."

"But Hickey killed him anyway."

"Big surprise. One of the Long family accountants is telling the Blackbirds that there's money enough to settle with them and that it's on its way."

"What do you think?"

"Beats me," I said. "But I do have an idea."

Chapter Forty-one

Assistant District Attorney Skip Wilder met me in the reception area and we walked together through the labyrinthian complex of the San Remo County District Attorney's offices.

The accommodations were spartan, small cubicles for the legal staff with even smaller ones for their assistants, all jammed together in the center of a warehouse-sized space whose walls were comprised of floor-to-ceiling green-tinted windows.

We made our way through the bullpen toward the back end of the warehouse where elegantly appointed, individually designed offices served to separate the executive staff from the grunts.

"He's none too happy today," Wilder said.

"I'm deeply saddened to learn that."

"Don't wise-mouth him, Buddy. He's in no mood."

We were met at his door by Michael Lytell's trusted assistant and, parenthetically, his wife, Nancy, both of whom I had known since boyhood. Small town.

Nancy Lytell came out from behind her desk and

gave me a hug. "Don't pay any attention to him," she said. "He's on one of his tears."

"Easy for you to say. You get to sit out here."

"How's Burton?"

"Good days and bad days."

"Will you send him our love?"

"Of course."

Michael Lytell emerged from the inner sanctum. He looked at me. "What, no uniform?"

"I don't believe in them."

"Figures."

He shook my hand weakly and led us inside.

"No calls," he said to Nancy, closing the door behind him.

He ushered us to the sitting area of his oversized office, a kind of conversation pit, with four armchairs and a sofa, all of them facing a wall of windows that presented a tinted overview of the Freedom foothills.

When we were seated, the District Attorney turned to me. "Your dime."

"And worth every penny," I answered.

He turned to Skip Wilder and said, "You see, already it starts."

"It's not my intention to aggravate you, Mike," I said. "But I'm preparing to take an action that will definitely upset you."

Lytell again turned to Skip Wilder.

"I told you," he said.

"Hear him out, Mike," Wilder said. "Give him a chance."

To me, Lytell said, "Go on."

"How much do you know about the Long family's connections to Oliver Darien?"

"You tell me."

"Are you aware of the size of their loss?"

"Not specifically."

"It's considerable."

"How considerable?"

"In confidence?"

Again he looked at Skip Wilder.

"He hasn't said one fucking thing and now he wants to swear me to confidence."

"Do it," Wilder said.

Lytell looked at me. "This better be good."

"Confidence?"

He sighed. "Yes."

"How does seventy million sound to you?"

"Like a goddamned lie."

"That's what I would have thought, too. But it's not."

"The Longs lost seventy million dollars with Oliver Darien?"

"It would appear so."

"Jesus. Where did they get that kind of money?"

"Good question."

"Do you know the answer?"

"Hickey Long was running drugs."

"Oh, please."

"He was. In fact, were you to go looking for him, you wouldn't find him because he's currently on the run from both the Blackbirds and the Sinaloan cartel."

Lytell was silent.

"Does Barry, Senior, know?" Wilder asked.

"Of course he knows. He masterminded the whole thing."

"These are some stiff allegations, Buddy," Lytell said. "I'm assuming you can back them up."

"That's why I'm here."

"To offer proof?"

"To make a proposal."

To Skip Wilder he said, "He's got no proof."

"Will you just shut up and listen to him?" Wilder shook his head.

"I need your cooperation," I said.

"In what?"

I told him.

Chapter Forty-two

It was the opening night of the three-day Heart of Our Saviour Celebration and the roads in and out of Freedom were jammed. License plates from nearly every state in the union and from Canada could be found in the Long Pavilion parking lot which, at nine a.m., was nearly filled.

Tailgate parties were underway and the air was rife with the aroma of grilled, smoked, and roasted meats. Although alcoholic beverages were technically forbidden, coolers packed with ice and beer were visible.

It was a brisk California day with an unseasonable chill in the air. Scarves and sweaters were in abundance. A number of bonfires, burning in large receptacles, attracted children who stood staring at the flames and senior citizens in search of warmth.

Food trucks of every stripe were up from L.A., ready to feed those who were not part of the tailgate culture. A Ferris wheel and several children's rides had been set up in a corner of the lot. A handful of midway games accompanied them.

Despite the festive atmosphere, many of the attendees could talk of nothing other than the Oliver Darien debacle and its impact on their beloved Reverend.

As was his custom on Celebration days, Barry Long, Junior, was in seclusion. Entrance to the family quarters was forbidden. Backstage passes for staff and crew were essential.

The Long family security team was out in full force, some stationed on the periphery of the Pavilion, others patrolling the parking lot. An elite force stood ready to tend to the Reverend and his family when they appeared.

At the County Courthouse, I greeted my team of deputies along with a cadre of police officers on loan from nearby townships that had been assigned to the Sheriff's Department for the duration of the festivities. The squad room was filled to overflowing with uniformed officers and plainclothes detectives, all armed, some brandishing stun guns and tear gas canisters.

Four groups of officers had assembled, each under the leadership of a Sheriff's Deputy, each poring over every detail of their assignments. At six p.m., they would deploy to Long Pavilion, where they would await the signal to move in.

Promptly at seven p.m., the convocation, as delivered by Pastor Leonard Handel, would keynote the Celebration.

I stood beside Johnny Kennerly and watched as the Heart of Our Saviour Choir performed several rousing spirituals that raised everyone's energy level. Celebrants stood and sang along with the choir. Several young people danced in the aisles.

Then came Barry Long the Third, all three and a half feet of him, who joined the choir in an upbeat rendition of "Nearer My God to Thee." The boy was dressed in a smartly tailored blue suit, adorned with a red-and-white polka-dotted bow tie.

He sang with childish enthusiasm, but without much skill. When the song was over, he bowed deeply, then ran off stage.

He was followed by his father, the Reverend Barry himself, whose entrance brought the crowd to its feet. The ovation went on for several minutes, during which the Reverend prowled the stage like some kind of feral beast, grabbing hands, touching foreheads, soaking up adoration as if it were his due.

He spoke for nearly an hour. His message was consistent with what I had seen on the DVD. He claimed to be a simple preacher whose devotion to those in need had earned him the ear of God. No mention was made of the financial debacle nor the vast sums of money that had been lost.

As he arrived at the pinnacle of his performance, with arms outstretched and eyes focused heavenward, he dropped to his knees and immersed himself in prayer.

Suddenly Barry Three toddled onto the stage and stood beside his father. He was quickly followed by Catharine, whose appearance brought the crowd to its feet in total frenzy. She wore a full-length white gown. She was pale and moved hesitantly, seemingly disoriented.

Reverend Barry strode swiftly to her side to assist. With their arms around each other, they walked to center stage. Barry Three ran to them and hugged tight to his mother. The family portrait complete, the Longs stood together, basking in the adoration of the assembled.

Catharine's entrance was the signal. Down each of the fourteen aisles marched two of my officers, led by Johnny Kennerly. They climbed onto the stage and swiftly moved to surround Catharine, who appeared even more confused and bewildered by what was taking place. Three remained glued to her side.

I watched Johnny produce an arrest warrant and hand it to Catharine Long. I couldn't hear what was being said but when I saw Johnny speaking directly to her, I knew he was reciting her rights.

Several officers ushered Catharine and Three from the stage, edging them toward the exit.

As the Reverend looked on, a number of Long family security guards moved as if to intercept the procession. They were stopped in their tracks by a rush of additional police officers.

A hush settled on the Pavilion as the faithful watched the unfolding events, uncertain as to what exactly was taking place.

Once Catharine, Three, and the officers were out of the building, the crowd erupted. Celebrants began yelling and stamping their feet. A number stood weeping. Several followed the officers outside and watched as they loaded Catharine and Three into one of the many squad cars that stood in wait.

Then, with sirens blaring, the vehicles raced off into the night.

Chapter Forty-three

In the chaos, accompanied by two Freedom police officers, Marsha Russo and I slipped backstage and headed for the family residence. The guard at the door was uncertain, but when we showed him our credentials, he stood aside.

The family quarters, located on ground level, were plush, filled with ultra-modern designer furniture and high-end electronic gadgetry.

We worked our way through the living area, den, dining room, and four separate bedrooms before arriving at the staff quarters located in the sub-basement level.

Utilitarian and spare, this area housed an industrial-sized kitchen plus three small offices, a common room, and a pair of tiny bathrooms.

We came upon a door bearing a sign that read *No Entry*.

When our master keys proved useless, I instructed one of the officers to shoot out the lock.

We pushed our way inside to a windowless great room, to be met by the alarmed stare of a small, nervous-looking, middle-aged man in rolled-up shirt-sleeves and loosened tie, wearing thick horn-rimmed glasses.

He was seated at a large oak desk, filled to overflowing with strewn papers and files. A number of large garbage bins, some half-filled with discarded paperwork, stood ready to receive more.

The room was a mess. Dozens of file cabinets, some with drawers hanging open like gaping maws, spit out a chaotic tangle of paper and file folders. Torn and emptied cardboard boxes filled the metal shelving units that lined the walls.

The man at the desk stood and glared at us. "This is private property."

"Not anymore it isn't."

The man removed a pinstriped, navy suit jacket from the back of his chair and put it on. He picked up a black leather briefcase from the floor beside him and made a move for the door.

"Would you be so good as to ID this person?" I said to the police officer who had accompanied us. "You might want to check him for any concealed weapons, as well."

The officer nodded and intercepted the wiry little man. "Wallet, please."

The man fished it out of his jacket pocket and handed it to the officer, who flipped through it. "Robert Albanis," the officer said to me.

"It's nice to meet you, Mr. Albanis. I'm Buddy Steel."

"What is it you want with me, Mr. Steel?"

"Sheriff Steel."

"Okay. What do you want with me, Sheriff Steel?"

"What is it you do here, Robert?"

"I prefer Bob," he said.

"Okay, Bob. What do you do here?"

"I work here."

"Doing what?"

"Stuff."

"What kind of stuff?"

"Accounting stuff."

"You're an accountant?"

"Yes."

"What exactly are you doing with these papers and file folders?"

"Destroying them."

"Because?"

"They're of no further use to us."

"To what do they relate?"

"They're business-related."

"And you're destroying them."

"Yes."

I glanced at Marsha Russo who shrugged.

"When exactly was it that you last spoke with Hickham Long?" I said to Bob Albanis.

"I beg your pardon?"

"When did he tell you he had a bead on the money?"

"I don't know what you're talking about."

"This isn't going well, Bob."

I turned to the police officer. "Would you please be so kind as to prepare Mr. Albanis for removal from the premises?"

Albanis became agitated. "What do you mean removal from the premises?"

"We're taking you with us," I said.

"You're not taking me anywhere. I'm an American citizen. I know my rights. I demand a phone call."

"And I'm sure you deserve one. But regardless of your citizenship, you get a phone call only if you've been arrested."

"What do you call this?"

"An anomaly."

"What's that supposed to mean?"

"It means you're not being arrested. You're being held for questioning."

"Questioning? What kind of questioning?"

"You'll find out."

"For how long?"

"For as long as it takes."

"You can't do this."

"You think?"

I nodded to the officer who took hold of Albanis' arm.

"I demand to know where you're taking me."

"Do you like to dance, Bob?" I asked.

"What do you mean dance?"

"Have you ever heard of the jailhouse shuffle?"

"What are you talking about? What in the fuck is the jailhouse shuffle?"

"You're about to find out."

Chapter Forty-four

We stashed Albanis in Victory, a small town on the northernmost tip of San Remo County, in one of the police station's four jail cells.

I wanted enough time to question him on my terms and the jailhouse shuffle provided a way to keep him in custody without an arrest being made or charges being filed. He would be moved on a daily basis, sometimes twice a day, throughout the county penal system, always one step ahead of any potential detection.

I left him to stew overnight about his current state of affairs and returned to Freedom. It wasn't more than fifteen minutes after I'd arrived when I heard a commotion in the squad room. Barry Long, Senior, and his attorney, Murray Kornbluth, were steaming in my direction.

Without waiting to be invited, they entered my office and planted themselves in front of me.

Kornbluth prided himself on the elegance of his attire. He had on a blue-and-gray pinstriped Armani suit, a Turnbull & Asser pale blue dress shirt, and a pink Gucci tie. His black loafers were Gucci, also. Were it not for his frenetic manner, his simian features, and his noticeable four o'clock shadow, he might actually have looked human.

"Where is she?" Droplets of spittle flew from the corners of his mouth.

I was all innocence, a study in curiosity. "Where is who?"

"Don't go there with me, Buddy," Kornbluth said. "I'm in no mood for your shenanigans."

Barry Long, Senior, demanded, "Where's my daughter-in-law?"

"They left."

"What, left?" Kornbluth said.

"I released them and they left."

"You released them to who?"

"To their own recognizance."

Enraged now, Kornbluth shouted, "You couldn't have. Where are they?"

I asked Marsha Russo to join us. When she did, I said, "Please tell their eminences here what took place with Mrs. Long."

"She left," Marsha said. "Deputy Sheriff Steel determined that neither she nor her son were a threat to flee, so he released them."

Both men stood speechless. They exchanged glances.

"Tell me where they went," Kornbluth insisted.

Marsha shrugged. "They didn't say."

Kornbluth whirled and faced me. "I don't believe a word of this, Buddy."

"Be that as it may, Murray, she's gone. And I'd like both of you to be gone as well."

Long Senior folded his arms across his chest. "I want to see for myself."

"Be my guest. Marsha, would you please give these two distinguished gentlemen the station tour? Allow them a peek at our currently unoccupied cell block. Then please escort them out."

Marsha nodded. "This way," she directed the two visitors.

Nearly apoplectic with rage, Kornbluth stomped out of the office followed by Long Senior.

Before closing the door after them, Marsha flashed me a look. "That was truly excellent."

A huge grin split her face.

Chapter Forty-five

Having made certain I wasn't being followed, I turned left onto Lewiston Street and parked the Wrangler a block and a half from Sarah Kaplow's house.

The patrol car that held Catharine Long and her son, Barry III, had furtively split from the main convoy and dropped them off at Sarah's, where they were greeted by a private-duty nurse, two security officers, and the indomitable librarian herself.

The nurse gave Catharine a hasty examination, and determined she was heavily sedated. She then put Catharine to bed. Barry III was a ball of fire, excited beyond measure to be reunited with his mother. The boy insisted he remain at Catharine's bedside, where he and Sarah spent the rest of their evening constructing a large Lego pirate ship.

"She'll be far more responsive in the morning," the nurse said. "Once the sedatives have worn off."

I asked Sarah to phone me when Catharine felt well enough to be interviewed. I explained that the security guards would be working eight-hour shifts and would inform her when each shift was about to change so she could familiarize herself with the next pair of officers.

"I've already told the library staff I'll be taking a few vacation days," Sarah said. "I want to be with her for as long as it's necessary."

"Once she's composed, we'll learn a lot more about what she wants to do."

I gave Sarah my cell number and the private line into the station, should she need to reach me. "I'll see you tomorrow."

"This was a clever idea, Buddy. For the life of me, though, I don't know how you got away with it."

"Can I tell you something, Sarah?"

She nodded.

"Neither do I."

We shared a laugh, then I left the house and went home to bed.

Chapter Forty-six

The next morning, with a sea of media splayed out in front of my condo, and having learned of a similar gathering at the County Courthouse, I decided not to conduct my interview with Catharine Long until the frenzy subsided.

Sarah Kaplow confirmed that Catharine was being examined by Dr. Lonnie MacDonald, Freedom's leading general practitioner, who would report his findings to me.

I slipped past the media and headed for Victory.

The desk sergeant led me to the cell where a visibly shaken Bob Albanis stared daggers at me.

"Morning, Bob," I said, cheerfully. "I trust the accommodations were to your satisfaction?"

"You have no right to hold me like this," he yelled. "I could have your badge for this."

"You're welcome to it. I don't usually carry it, anyway."

"Are you mouthing wise with me, Mr. Steel?"

"Why would you say a thing like that?"

"What is it you want?"

I shrugged. "I'm prepared to make you a one-time-only offer, Bob. So you'll be wanting to listen carefully. You tell me what I want to know and your life will become immeasurably better."

"What do you want to know?"

"Everything."

"Such as?"

"What was in the file cabinets?"

"What file cabinets?"

"That's not the right answer, Bob."

"I don't know what you mean."

"What was in the files you were destroying?"

"What files?"

"You're not making me happy, Bob. And the most important thing in your life right now is making me happy. *Comprende?* I'm going to ask you one more question. If you answer incorrectly, your future will be considerably less bright. Am I clear? Now tell me, why was the office being dismantled?"

It took Albanis several moments to accept this new reality. Finally he said, "Because we were told to dismantle it."

"By whom?"

He looked at me but didn't speak.

"By whom, Bob?"

"By Hickham Long."

"Why?"

"He didn't say."

"What was in the file cabinets?"

"Lots of stuff. Financials, mostly."

"What kind of financials?"

"Sales records. Balance sheets. Monthly statements. That kind of stuff."

"What kind of statements?"

"Income. Expenditures."

"What were you going to do with them?"

"Hickey wanted them torched."

"So you burned them."

"Yes."

"Did you duplicate them?"

"He wouldn't let me. He didn't want to leave any traces behind."

Albanis stared at me in an effort to gauge my response to his story. When he realized I was watching him intently, he looked away.

"You're a CPA, right?"

"I am."

"For the Longs?"

"They're my only client."

"And you were destroying financial records at their behest."

"Something like that."

"I want to know everything about the records you destroyed. I want copies of them. I also want the names of everyone connected with the operation."

"I just told you, Hickey ordered me to destroy all of that information."

"I'm not here to play footsie with you, Bob. I'm betting that whatever it was Hickey Long ordered you to do, you managed to defy him."

He remained silent.

"I want everything you have on the Longs, including their involvement with the Blackbirds. I want the names of the distribution team. The guys who push the junk around the neighborhoods. I also want information as to how they operated with Oliver Darien, how the money was laundered, and how Darien was able to bamboozle them. And I want the paper trail that proves it. And the cherry on the cake, Bob? I want to know where Hickey is right now and what money he has a bead on."

"And if I provide you with this information?"

"You win a Get Out of Jail Free card."

"What if I wanted more than that?"

"What more?"

"Witness protection."

"You want to go underground?"

"If I were to provide you with the information you're seeking, my life wouldn't be worth a plugged nickel."

I thought about that for a while. "Okay."

"Okay what?"

"You give me everything I'm asking for, I'll deliver WitPro."

"How do I know?"

"Know what?"

"That you'll keep your word."

"You don't."

"Then why would I do it?"

"Because it's your only play." I grinned at him and stood. "I'll be back for your answer."

As I headed for the door, Albanis leapt to his feet and grabbed hold of the cell bars with both hands. He pressed his face between them.

"When? When will you be back?"

I waved to him over my shoulder and left.

Chapter Forty-seven

When I arrived at my office, Marsha told me my father was in the building and looking for me. I took the stairs two at a time.

He was seated behind his desk, a faraway look in his eyes. It took him a few moments to focus on me.

"Buddy," he said.

"Morning, Dad. How you doing today?"

"Not too bad. Just a little bit of trouble with my hands. Nothing works like it used to."

His longtime assistant, Lesley Berson, inquired as to whether I might like some coffee, which I did. After pouring me a cup, she tended to the Sheriff, making certain he was comfortable. When she was satisfied, she slipped quietly out of the room.

"There's some news," my father said.

"Okay."

"From Grand Cayman Island."

I waited for him to continue.

"A body washed ashore this morning. It had been floating for at least a couple of days and was pretty bloated. The Cayman police ran checks on the hotels and the major airlines but drew blanks. There's a small alternate terminal on the island. Lots of private air traffic in and out."

"And?"

"Three days ago a Gulfstream IV flew in with a single passenger. Guy called Oliver Darien, Junior. The Cayman authorities believe the body was his."

"Darien must have kept a stash in one of the banks down there."

"He did."

"Do we know which one?"

"We do now. The Darien family had several accounts and a pair of safe deposit boxes at The First Federal Bank of Grand Cayman, a privately owned facility."

"What do they say?"

"At first they said nothing. But after I got done speaking with the bank's senior officer, they agreed to cooperate."

"Still got it, eh, Dad?"

The old man's face flushed with excitement. His efforts on the case temporarily rejuvenated him. For the first time in a long while, he was himself.

"The First Fed produced a security tape filmed when Oliver Darien, Junior, showed up to withdraw funds. I'm in possession of that tape, thanks in large part to the Freedom Police techies who understand the concept of streaming video."

"Were you planning to show it to me?"

"It's all racked and ready to go."

I stood behind him and watched over his shoulder. A picture of three men, two of them with their backs to the camera, was frozen on his computer screen. My father pressed the Return key and the picture came to life.

The man facing the camera was handing a large leather satchel to one of the other two men, after which they all shook hands. The two men then turned in the direction of the camera.

Just before they exited the frame, my father froze the picture again, this time revealing their faces. One of the men was likely Oliver Darien, Junior. The other was Hickham Long.

"We'll, I'll be damned," I said.

"Hickey, right?"

"Exactly." I felt a sharp twinge in my shoulder. I rubbed it for several moments, then sat back down and finished my coffee. After a while, I said, "Murder."

"Darien, Junior?"

"Hickey must have extracted the information he was seeking from Darien, Senior, and then used it to track down the son."

"And they flew to Grand Cayman."

"In cahoots," I said.

"Because?"

"Both of them were desperate. The money Darien kept in the Caymans had to have been all that was left. I'm guessing they made a deal to split it."

"Why would Darien, Junior, make such a deal?"

"He didn't have a whole lot of choice. He knew the scam was over and he had to get his hands on whatever was left before the story broke and the dough was frozen. Hickey knew it, too. He tortured the information out of the old man, then raced down to L.A. to intercept Junior."

"Who didn't yet know about what happened to his father."

"Exactly."

"Which is why he was willing to go along with Hickey."

"Hickey knew he couldn't access the money without Junior. Junior knew the extent of Hickey's losses, and more than likely, feared him. He must have figured that splitting the stash was his best option."

"He didn't realize he was signing his own death certificate," my father mused while dabbing a speck of spittle from the corner of his mouth.

"Not hardly."

We sat quietly for a while.

Then I said, "So, if the two of them take a private plane to Grand Cayman, why do the manifests report only a single passenger?"

Without missing a beat, my father commented, "Corruption."

"Doesn't the crew have to report all passengers to the Customs officials?"

"Not if there's enough money to thwart them."

"Which Hickey had once he got his hands on Darien's stash. Did your contact tell you how much there was in the accounts?"

"Somewhere shy of a million. But he didn't know anything about the contents of the safe deposit boxes."

"Which had to have held enough for Hickey to buy off the local authorities. And when he delivers it here, it should also be enough to get the Birds off his back."

"How much, would you guess?"

I thought about it for a few moments. "Another million, give or take."

My father nodded. "That would be my guess."

"Did the same plane fly him out?" I asked.

"Out of the Caymans?"

"Yes."

"There's no record of his leaving."

"You mean he's still there?"

"I wouldn't think so. There are a whole lot of ways you can slip out of the Caymans. Especially if you have some dough."

"I'm thinking it's time to rein him in," I said.

"If you can find him."

"There's that."

The Sheriff stirred and shifted uncomfortably in his chair. "I tend to tire easily."

"May I take you home?"

"Lesley will. Thanks just the same."

"Shall I call her?"

"In a minute. I'm sorry about all this, Buddy."

"About what?"

"This mess I dumped on you."

"You didn't dump anything on me, Dad. Don't beat yourself up. This case will get solved. The shit will resolve itself and everything will go back to normal. Whatever normal is."

"For what it's worth, I think you're doing a very good job."

"Nothing you wouldn't have done better. But I'm grateful you said it."

Chapter Forty-eight

Wilma put Sarah Kaplow through to me.

"You better come over here, Buddy," Sarah said.

"What's wrong?"

"She is."

"What's that supposed to mean?"

"Best you come over."

I took all the back roads and got there within twenty minutes. No one followed me.

Sarah greeted me at the door and ushered me into her den, a wood-paneled room crammed full with wall-to-wall bookcases and unremarkable mismatched furniture, all of it worn and comfortable-looking.

Catharine Long was wearing jeans and a sweater, sipping tea. She was no longer sedated but appeared uneasy and anxious. She was much younger-looking in person than she appeared in the videos. "It's nice to finally meet you," I said.

She focused on me. "You're that Sheriff, right?" I nodded. "You certainly captured the attention of the Longs. You shook up every one of them."

She seemed unsettled, distracted, as if she were wrestling with herself internally. Then she bolted upright, as though she had reached some kind of decision.

She spoke directly to Sarah Kaplow. "I have to leave here, Sarah. Now. I'm going on tonight. I'm appearing at the Celebration. With my son and my husband."

Sarah was taken aback. "Why would you do that?"

"It's my duty."

"After all they did to you?"

"You mean after all my father-in-law and brother-in-law did to me?"

I interrupted her. "You don't believe your husband played a role in your kidnapping?"

"I don't want to talk about that."

"Are you suggesting he didn't know you were being held captive?"

"I'm not suggesting anything. Right now I have an obligation to my followers. I intend to fulfill that obligation. Are you planning to also hold me against my will, Sheriff?"

"You're free to do anything you want, Mrs. Long. But not holding your husband accountable for the manner in which you were treated is a terrible mistake."

After several moments, she thoughtlessly delivered a rote response. "I'll take it under advisement."

"That's your privilege. But I'm not through with him. He was a participant in some pretty despicable behavior. Behavior I wouldn't describe as *deeply spiritual.* Guys like him sweep their corruption under the nearest apology and beg forgiveness for it. More than likely you'll see a repeat performance, Mrs. Long. You've already played victim. For sure, you'll play it again."

"Thank you for sharing your opinion, Mr. Steel. Now, if it's all right with you, I'd like to return to the Pavilion."

"My deputy will escort you."

"Thank you." She turned abruptly and left the library. Sarah Kaplow watched her go.

"Why didn't you try to stop her?"

"It wouldn't have made any difference. You heard her. She's got an obligation to her followers. She's caught up in the drama. Particularly since she's such an integral part of it."

"I suppose."

"She's very young, Sarah."

"Also a factor."

A sarcastic smile insinuated itself onto my face. "And lest we forget, *there's no business like show business.*"

"You're so cynical, Buddy."

"Who, me?"

"Yes, you."

"With good reason."

"It's your Achilles heel, you know."

"Cynicism?"

"Yes."

"Why would you say a thing like that?"

"Because I know you. I watched you grow up, remember. Who better than me to call you out?"

Catharine Long stepped back into the library. Her son and the nurse stood behind her in the hallway.

"Thank you for everything, Sarah," she said.

"You're sure you want to do this, Catharine?"

"More than you'll ever know."

Mrs. Long peered in my direction, but refused to make eye contact. She stepped back and picked up her son and nuzzled his hair. "We're going to see Daddy now."

"I don't want to see Daddy," the boy cried, flailing his arms about. "I hate Daddy."

She embraced him in an attempt to calm him. "No you don't."

"Yes, I do," the boy screamed. "I do. I do. I do. I hate him. I hate my Daddy. I never want to see him again."

His rant became louder and more chaotic.

Catharine put him down and as soon as she did, the boy lashed out at her, slapping at her with his fists, trying also to kick her.

The nurse lifted him up, which alarmed him. He started to sob. Catharine took him and clutched him to her chest. She began gently patting his back.

With the boy still in her arms, she stepped quickly to Sarah Kaplow and knelt beside her. "Don't underestimate me, Sarah. This is far from over."

She gave Sarah a quick peck on the cheek, glanced sideways at me, then left the house.

Chapter Forty-nine

Although my father and Her Honor had invited me to live in their mansion, I wanted distance between us, so I sublet a condo in the foothills. Despite its meager furnishings and bleak surroundings, I like it.

It has two bedrooms, a living-dining room combo, a full-sized kitchen, and two bathrooms. The landlord provided furnishing for only one bedroom, so the second one stands empty, used only when I'm given to fits of pacing.

With the exception of the master bedroom, which overlooks the low-lying mountains, the rest of the views are of the neighboring streets and houses.

The living room does open onto a small terrace, big enough for a lounge chair and a side table, and offering a blast of direct sunlight that it receives for the better part of an hour each day at around noon.

The utilitarian gray concrete building holds six units, with parking spaces for them in the rear. There's a small outdoor swimming pool and an even smaller exercise room that contains four stationary bikes, two treadmills, and a weight machine.

I swung the Wrangler into the driveway, past the diminished throng of media personnel, heading for my parking space when I spotted her.

She was sitting on a small, grassy knoll, wearing a fisherman's cap and a thick woolen pea coat, resembling a weather-beaten sailor after a hurricane. She looked up as I drove by and when I jammed on the brakes, she slung a small duffel over her shoulder, ambled to the Wrangler, and climbed in.

She planted a wet kiss on my cheek and said, "The damsel rescued from near-certain hypothermia shows her appreciation."

"Not good enough."

"How not good enough?"

"The level of gratitude is far too meager."

"I trust we'll be going indoors once you park this sucker, correct?"

"Correct."

She removed the fisherman's cap and shook out her hair. "The level of gratitude will elevate even more significantly once we're indoors."

I parked and although several members of the media had noticed us, we managed to duck inside before they could swarm.

She dropped her duffel on the upholstered two-seater in the living room and poked around the place, looking into each of the rooms. After the inspection, she watched me fix a pair of gin and tonics. "I took a chance."

"On?"

"Your being hospitable."

"How'm I doing?"

"Better than expected."

"What are you doing here, Maggie?"

She removed the pea coat and ran her fingers through her rich auburn hair, which she nervously swept off her forehead. She had on a long-sleeved, blue man's dress shirt worn over a pair of black tights. Clearly she was bra-less and she noticed me trying not to notice.

She plunked herself down on the sofa. "I'm in the shits, Buddy. There's no one else I can talk to."

I handed her the gin, picked up one of the straight-back chairs from the dining table, placed it in front of her and sat. "So, talk."

"It's worse than I imagined. And you playing Javert isn't helping."

"Go on."

"This business with Oliver Darien has brought my father to his knees. He's angry all the time. He never stops talking but he says nothing. My brother, Barry, has become despondent. His life has come crashing down. He's estranged from Catharine. The kid can't stand him. And worse, he can't stand the kid."

Once started, she could barely stop talking long enough to take a breath. "He's constantly beleaguered by creditors. He's tried his best to maintain his piety, but after your raid, he lost it. And of course you know Hickey's vanished. Allegedly with blood on his hands. Could things get any worse?"

"They could if you were a part of it."

"Unintended consequences is my part."

"Meaning?"

"Over time, I managed to squirrel away a little nest

egg from the financial support my father provided. Without it I'd be totally broke."

The realization dawned on me that despite her declarations to the contrary, she was still attached to her family. I dropped the most recent bombshell on her. "At least there's now a measure of consolation for the Reverend."

This last caught her attention. "Which is?"

"Catharine went back to him."

She gasped. "She went back to him? To Barry?"

"Yep."

"When? Today?"

"Yep."

"Why would she do that?"

"Exactly my question to her."

"To which she replied?"

"Some bullshit about family first."

I watched as she considered her response. "Despite what she went through?"

"Because of what she went through."

"She's as crazy as the rest of them."

Again I held her gaze. A brief silence settled over us before I asked a second time, "So why are you here?"

"In Freedom or with you?"

"In Freedom."

"Barry asked me to come."

"Senior or Junior?"

"Both."

"Why?"

"Senior needed a shoulder to cry on and I was the only one of his offspring he could count on."

"And Junior?"

"To complain about Senior."

I got up and began pacing, wondering what was really going on between her and her family. After a while I said, "And with me?"

"I don't know, Buddy. I'm not in a good place. I don't know what to do."

"And you think I can help?"

"I'm here, aren't I?"

She drained her drink. I fixed us both another and when I came back, she was softly crying. "This was a mistake. I'll finish my drink and leave."

"You don't have to do that."

"I have no business dumping on you like this. We hardly know each other. I've put too much emotional weight on the brief time we spent together. I apologize."

I stopped pacing and stood in front of her. "I think about you."

She looked at me. "What about your ethics?"

"They trouble me. If I were a saner person, I'd have never let you in here."

"But you did."

"Which I'm certain I'll live to regret."

She shook her head. "I told you I was trouble."

"But you never said how much."

"Do you want me to leave?"

"Yes and no."

"Not a good enough answer."

"Yes, then."

She allowed that to sink in for a few moments. She gulped down a fair measure of gin, stood, and muttered, "Okay, I'm out of here."

She grabbed her duffel, shot me a withering glance, and headed for the door. Then she stopped dead in her tracks. Dropping the duffel, she made a beeline for me. She leapt at me and threw her arms around my neck.

"This is so crazy," she murmured.

She kissed me with a great deal of urgency. I kissed her back. She broke away to say, "What is this about?"

"You tell me."

"Time out of time?"

"I suppose that's one way of looking at it."

"Can you think of anything better?"

"I can't think of anything at all just now."

We left a trail of clothing on our way to the bedroom. We abandoned rationality and went at each other with ferocity and tenderness, plus a child-like sense of discovery. Each time we thought we had hit the heights, we found new ones.

Dawn was breaking when we finally slept.

Chapter Fifty

By ten o'clock, I'd already shaved, showered, and dressed. The coffee was made and I was removing the toast from the oven when she wandered into the kitchen, wearing one of my t-shirts, still wiping the sleep from her eyes.

"Amazing," she said.

"What is?"

"That anyone can function on so little sleep."

"Do I look like I'm functioning?"

"A whole lot better than I am."

She slathered a wad of unsalted butter on her sourdough toast and poured two heaping spoonfuls of sugar in her coffee.

"Ugh," I said.

"And your objection is?"

"Butter and sugar."

"You put them on the table."

"Only for show."

"You should have said something."

She chomped down the toast and took a large slurp of coffee. "I gather you're going out."

"Meetings."

"I'm not ready to leave just yet."

"No matter. Close the door behind you. It locks itself."

"I mean I'm not ready to leave Freedom. I'd like to stay here."

"You mean you want to move in?"

"Not in that sense. I want to stay in Freedom for a few more days to keep an eye on my father. Is that a problem for you?"

I thought it more politic if I didn't answer that particular question. Turns out I was wrong. She jumped all over me. "It is, isn't it? Is it an ethical problem or a commitment problem?"

"Both."

"Swell. Listen, Buddy, I'll be gone by the time you get home. But allow me to tell you something. I can sympathize with your ethical problem. I might even be able to comprehend your commitment issues. But apart from some serious self-evaluation, you might want to step outside of yourself and take into consideration that I might have a few ethical problems of my own."

I waited silently for the other shoe to drop.

"Just for the record here, big boy, I'd like you to understand that life as we knew it is no longer a reality for me and my family. My father has led us to financial ruin. My idiot brother dealt narcotics and maybe even murdered a few people. My pious asshole brother is wallowing in self-pity with no viable exit strategy.

"And in case you're interested, I, who has devoted her life to having nothing to do with any of them, have now become the family mediator. Whatever level of independence I believed I had earned has proven illusory. I misjudged the difference between financial assistance and indentured servitude. In other words, Buddy, I'm fucked. With the exception of a tiny reserve, I'm as busted as the rest of them.

"And if that wasn't enough, for some unknown reason I have these feelings for you. Am I totally neurotic or what?"

She retreated inside herself for several moments, then went on. "Let me ask you a dumb question."

"How dumb?

"Dumb enough. What do you feel for me?"

"What do I feel?"

"Oh, come on, Buddy. Just answer the question."

I found myself stumped, adrift in uncertainty.

She glared at me. "I'm waiting."

"I'm conflicted."

"Great answer, Buddy. You may be the only person I know who's more frightened of commitment than I am. You think I'm trouble? You're every bit my equal."

"There's the ethical thing, too."

"Fuck the ethical thing. You're not the only one of us with ethical issues. What really scares you is that if you allow yourself to have genuine feelings for someone, you believe you're going to get stepped on." She shook her head. "Am I welcome to stay here or not?"

I continued to dither for several moments before finally answering, "Yes."

"Yes, what?"

"Yes, you're welcome to stay here."

A small smile revealed itself at the corners of her mouth. "Now that wasn't so hard, was it?"

"It was brutal."

"Get over it."

Chapter Fifty-one

We moved Bob Albanis from Victory to the town of Vista Loma, in the southernmost part of the county. He was grumpy and agitated when I showed up.

I stood in front of his cell, a small windowless space, dank and unfriendly. A cot with an uncased pillow and a rough wool blanket, plus a hard wooden chair were the only pieces of furniture. A sink and a toilet stood in the corner. Overhead lighting fixtures burned ceaselessly.

"Hidey Ho, Bobby," I said. "Sleep well?"

"Spare me your wise-ass mouth, Steel. You're holding me against my will."

"And I feel terrible about it."

"Fuck you, too."

"What's your decision?"

"Yes."

"Yes what?"

"I'll do it."

"I was counting on you to say that."

"I'll need my computer."

"Where is it?"

"Hidden."

"Where?"

"In a safe place."

"You scanned them, didn't you?"

"Yes."

"And Hickey didn't know."

"Fuck Hickey."

"Where?"

"Same place as the names and the other stuff you want."

"They're on a computer?"

"A tablet."

"Where?"

"I'll take you there."

I thought about his offer for several moments. "How do I know you're not lying?"

"Because new best friends don't lie to each other."

• • ● • •

We loaded Albanis into a police van, his wrists bound and his ankles shackled, the chains hooked to a steel ring embedded in the floor of the van.

He whined. "Why?"

"A safeguard."

"A safeguard from what?"

"From you bolting and disappearing into the woods."

"As if I would do such a thing."

"Alas, we'll never know."

We were buzzed through the gates and proceeded up the winding driveway to the motor court in front of the Long family mansion.

A brisk Santa Ana wind stirred the foliage that fronted the elaborate portico. A murder of crows cavorted loudly among the aspens and maples.

P.J. Lincoln and Johnny Kennerly escorted Albanis from the van to the front porch where we were met by a genial, gray-haired black man of a certain age, in butler's yellow-and-black livery, a quizzical look on his face.

"How may I help you gentlemen?"

"We're assisting Mr. Albanis."

"Assisting him?"

"That's correct."

"In what?"

"That would be Sheriff's business. Mr. Albanis wishes to visit his office."

"Sheriff's business?"

"Yes."

"You're a Sheriff?"

"San Remo County."

"How come you're not dressed like a Sheriff?"

"I'm posing a challenge to the norm."

The elderly butler reached into his pocket and produced a pair of thick-lensed spectacles. He put them on and examined me closely. "I don't have to let you in here, you know."

"Are you new to this job, Mr....?"

"George. Just George will do."

"Are you?"

"New? No, sir. I've been with Mr. Long, Senior, since 2009."

"And now you're here?"

"Personnel reduction and redeployment. Hopefully temporary."

"Hopefully. Are you familiar with Mr. Albanis?"

"I am."

"He's here to visit his office. May we enter?"

The butler reserved judgment for several moments, then, with a cagey grin on his face, he stepped aside. "Please do."

"Thank you, George. I believe Mr. Albanis knows the way."

Shackled and slow-moving, Bob Albanis led me to the small elevator that took us to his office, located among the rooms on the top floor. He unlocked the door and I followed him inside. P.J. and Johnny waited in the hall.

It was a compact room facing the sea, and the morning sun poured through a large dormer window. Several file cabinets, a desk, and two chairs comprised all of the room's furniture.

Albanis gave his office the once-over, then he led us to the men's bathroom located at the end of the hall. He stepped directly to one of the room's two toilets and reached behind the back of its water tank.

He fumbled around for a while, his movements hampered as a result of his hands being bound together. His frustration mounting, he turned to me and grumbled, "You do it."

I reached behind the tank and located an item affixed to it by means of heavy-duty duct tape. I stripped the tape from the tank and freed the object which proved to be an iPad.

"That's it," Albanis said.

I attempted to activate it, but all that appeared on the screen was a sketch of a battery with a large red X drawn through it.

"It needs to be charged," Albanis said.

"Okay."

Still holding the iPad, I stepped back into the hall. "We're on the move," I said to Johnny and P.J.

We encountered George, the butler, on our way to the van. "Find what you were looking for?"

"No. Mr. Albanis now believes he may have left it elsewhere."

The elderly butler shook his head and lamented, "That's a shame."

"It's always something," I agreed.

The sly grin reappeared on George's weathered face. "Tell me about it."

Once in the van, we headed for the County Courthouse.

"What happens now?" Albanis queried, fishing for information in the officious manner of the professional CPA that he was.

"We examine the contents of the iPad."

"And me?"

"You get to enjoy the Jailhouse Shuffle for a bit longer."

"I need access to my cell phone."

"Why?"

"If you want to know where Hickey is, I have to check the number he called from."

"Where is your phone?"

"At the Pavilion."

"Where?"

"Hidden."

"Where?"

"You won't find it."

I turned to face Johnny. "Change of plan. We're going to the Pavilion."

• • ● • •

Albanis was right. I would never have found it. It was secreted behind a loose brick in a corner of the backstage green room. The still-handcuffed accountant pointed it out and I pried the brick loose, reached inside, and found the phone.

The battery was low but still functional. At Albanis' direction, I entered his password and once in, accessed his recent call list and scrolled down until he told me to stop at a call labeled *Blocked.*

When I attempted to return the call, all I could ascertain was that it had originated from a 305 area code, which now went unanswered. 305 is the code for Miami, Florida.

"So he made it out of the Caymans and got himself to Miami," I concluded.

"Seems like it," Albanis agreed.

"Where would he be in Miami?"

"He could be anywhere. But I'm guessing he's on his way here."

I wondered again about Albanis' relationship to Hickey and whether he knew more about Hickey's movements than he was letting on. "You're suggesting that he's coming to Freedom?"

"Yes."

"Because?"

"Unfinished business."

"Regarding?"

"Let's just leave it at that, shall we?"

"If I'm not mistaken, you're still angling for the WitPro option, am I right about that?"

Albanis didn't say anything.

I chided him. "This might be the right moment for you to ratchet up the cooperation level, Bob. If you value your future, that is."

I left him in the care of Marsha Russo at the courthouse jail in Freedom.

"I want you to employ all of your vast knowledge and skill to squeeze him dry," I told her. "Go for it."

"Meaning?"

"I want to know everything. He's primed to give it all up. It's up to you to yank it out of him."

"How will I know if he's telling the truth?"

"Polygraph."

"Not always reliable."

"If in doubt, threaten the son of a bitch."

"With what?"

"Make something up."

"You know what, Buddy?" Marsha said. "You are some piece of business."

"Thank you."

"It wasn't meant as a compliment."

Chapter Fifty-two

Once I had deposited Albanis with Marsha, I sought out Sheriff's Deputy Al Striar and handed him the iPad.

He examined it front to back, open and closed. "What have we here?"

"It belongs to Bob Albanis."

"The accountant?"

"One and the same. He claims to have scanned all the paperwork that Hickey Long instructed him to destroy and downloaded it onto that tablet."

He stared at the iPad and began turning it in his hands again. Then he looked at me.

"The battery's low," I said. "Charge the sucker and transfer the contents to our mainframe and print them out. Have a look. If what he says is true, there could be enough information in those spreadsheets and financials to deep-fry Long's geese."

"Got it."

"See if you can track down Dave Richardson."

"The Department CPA?"

"Yeah, him. Ask him to have a look, too. If the financials are as revealing as Albanis says, it would be good to have an accounting professional from our side examine them. Eventually they'll wind up in forensics, but at the outset, I want a trained eye telling me what they signify."

"Okay."

"Oh, and ask Johnny to run the names. Albanis took great pains to preserve them. I'm particularly interested in the distribution network. The Birds. Their guys on the street. Everyone."

"When do you want this confirmation?"

"How about yesterday? Would yesterday morning work for you?"

Striar rolled his eyes. "I wish you were as amusing as you think you are."

• • ● • •

"And if it's conclusive?" my father asked.

We were sitting on the sun porch. He hadn't felt up to traveling to the office and had asked me to meet him at the house.

"It's the ammunition we need to go after Barry Long the First."

"Will it be enough to indict?"

"That's a question for the District Attorney."

"What is it you want from me?"

"If the tablet holds all the information Albanis claims it does, I'm going to need to help him go bye-bye."

"WitPro?"

"Exactly."

"Feds will have to arrange that."

"I know."

"You want me to talk to them?"

"You're the Sheriff."

"And if they say no?"

"They can't say no."

"They can say anything they want. They're the federal government."

"They won't say no to you."

"You give me too much credit."

"Humility doesn't suit you, Burton. Just make it happen, okay? I've already put it on the table."

"Without speaking with me first?"

"Yes."

"Presumptuous little bastard, aren't you?"

"The tree doesn't stand too far from the fallen apple."

"I'll see what I can do."

"That's decent of you."

"Was it your intention to piss me off today, Buddy?"

"Not at the outset."

"When did it change?"

"When you climbed onto your high horse."

"I'm guessing you can find your way out."

"Make this happen, will you please, Sheriff?"

He stared daggers at me. "I said I'd see what I can do."

Chapter Fifty-three

It was the closing night of the Heart of Our Saviour Revival Celebration and the Pavilion was packed. Catharine Long's arrest, plus the release of the Ponzi scheme story, brought renewed focus on the Long family. A goodly number of the faithful turned out in support of the Reverend.

I stood in the back of the arena, watching the show and the audience, which was on its feet, swaying and singing along with the choir, seated in hushed silence when Three again performed "Nearer My God to Thee," then leaping to its collective feet as he bowed deeply.

Reverend Barry held them in thrall and when Catharine appeared on stage, the crowd went wild. After she delivered a moving and heartfelt homily, the three Longs stepped off the stage and walked among the gathering, which parted lovingly for them.

I spotted Barry the First, standing in front of the stage, a self-satisfied grin on his puffy face. Next to him, her arm linked with his, stood Maggie.

I watched them for a while. They appeared quite intimate. The elder Barry whispered frequently in his daughter's ear, which elicited a galaxy of responses, from smiles and hugs, to frowns and concerned looks. There seemed to be no tension between them. They looked comfortable in each other's orbit.

Contrary to expectations, despite the media revelations regarding Oliver Darien and the questions surrounding Hickham Long, the Celebration was a success. The proceeds would surely bolster the family coffers, helping them sidestep further financial disaster, at least for the short term.

The procession exited the arena, followed in short order by Barry Senior and Maggie. I suppose I couldn't blame her for being there. I understood why she decided to show the flag, so to speak. She had referred to herself as the family mediator. If their fortunes were aided by the success of the Celebration, she stood to benefit financially.

As for me, despite the appearance of familial devotion between them, it was still my intention to complete the investigation. An intention that had begun to raise feelings of guilt in me.

Although she was aware of my suspicions regarding her brother and her father, she didn't know how close I was to bringing them down—an act that would seriously impact her because the Feds were sure to step in and seize their assets. I was certain she'd blame me for their downfall.

Hours later, when she arrived at my condo, I was in the living room, a newly cracked bottle of gin already half empty, my spirits low.

"Buddy," she called out, closing the door behind her.

"Over here."

"Why are you sitting in the dark?"

She switched on a lamp, enveloping the room in a blanket of somber light. She stared at me. I looked back at her through an alcohol haze.

She spoke first. "What?"

"It was a surprise to see you reunited with your father."

"You were there?"

"I wouldn't have missed it."

"Jesus."

"That's all you can say?"

"I had no choice."

I nodded and looked away.

She snarled at me. "You don't agree?"

"It's not what I expected from you."

"What you expected from me? How could you have an expectation of anything I would or would not do?"

"Obviously, I was wrong."

"How dare you sit in judgment of me."

"Judgment?"

"That's right. You sit in your holier than thou Sheriff's effluvium and pass judgment on those who don't measure up to your lofty expectations."

I took another pull of gin.

"Keep in mind that you're currently blitzed," she said. "That's not what I expected from you."

She stood and began to pace nervously, darting in and out of the light, moving close to me, then ducking quickly away. "We appear to have reached an impasse, you and I. You think I'm unprincipled. I believe you're at war with your so-called ethics."

She stopped pacing and stood staring at me. "I have this nagging feeling I may be in love with you, Buddy. How's that coming from someone who's as fearful of commitment as you are? Is it because we're such a perfect fit that we're behaving like misfits?"

She walked into the bedroom and moments later emerged, the duffel slung over her shoulder. She dropped the key on the hall table.

"Thanks for letting me stay here." She closed the door behind her.

I finished the gin and passed out where I sat, never bothering to switch off the lamp.

Chapter Fifty-four

It took three cups of coffee and four Advil to ease my hangover. I arrived at the office later than usual. Marsha Russo stared at me with a raised eyebrow. I ignored her and headed for my office. She followed.

"Looks like someone had a bit of a soggy night," she said.

"It's that noticeable?"

"The red eyes are the tell. You look like a tree frog."

"Was that all you wanted?"

"Actually, no."

"What, then?"

"It's the girl, isn't it?"

"What girl?"

"Don't play all innocent with me, Buddy. It's Margaret de Winter. Right?"

"Why would you think that?"

"Feminine intuition. Does she know what you're up to?"

"I don't know."

"Come on, Buddy. You're angling to bring down the whole kit and kaboodle. Does she know?"

"It's likely."

A testy silence enveloped us. I knew all too well that Marsha had my best interests at heart. Regardless of whether or not I agreed with her.

"How do you feel about her?"

"How do I feel?"

"Quit evading."

"I have feelings for her."

"Do you love her?"

"Maybe. If I understood what that meant."

"Don't blindside her, Buddy."

"Was there something specific you wanted to see me about, Marsha?"

"Striar and Richardson await an audience."

"Regarding the files?"

"They didn't say. May I invite them to join us?"

I nodded.

She picked up the phone and rang Al Striar on the intercom. He and Dave Richardson quickly appeared in my doorway.

Dave carried a laptop computer and placed it in front of me. He and Striar stepped behind me and Dave reached over and pressed the keys that opened the spreadsheet file.

I frowned. "What am I looking at?"

"A network of interconnecting numerical data that points to a single conclusion."

"Could you speak English, please, Dave?"

"They're knee-deep in it."

"In what?"

"The data purports that over the course of the last twelve months, a significant amount of Long family capital was invested in the purchase and distribution of crystal methamphetamine, which netted a considerable profit. On top of that is additional income assumed to have been generated by the Darien Financial Group."

"The scam."

"On paper the profits appeared huge. Especially since Darien was reporting that their funds were generating greater-than-market revenues.

"Darien didn't question the source of their investments, so the Longs believed that when it came time to cash out, their ill-gotten gains would magically turn into legitimate profits. With no one any the wiser. Those boys must have been as happy as pigs in shit.

"Then it turns out the setup was a fraud. The scammers became the scammed. And their roof caved in."

"That information is contained in the files?"

"As glaring as your red eyes."

I blinked and looked up at him. "That noticeable, eh?"

"Like Dracula on steroids."

"That's funny, Dave. Tell me again."

"The Longs were using Oliver Darien to launder their drug money. Hallelujah and praise the profits. Until the Feds blew the whistle on Darien's Ponzi scheme, which cost them every penny they believed they owned."

"Is this a great country, or what?" I said. "Do these files prove their involvement?"

"Almost."

"Almost what?"

"All we need to complete the circle are the cancelled checks that match the data. Checks signed by any one of the Longs, but preferably by Barry Senior."

"How do we get these checks?"

"We pay an official visit to the executive offices of The Bank of Northern California, Freedom branch, home to all of the Long family business and personal accounts."

"Okay."

"We request copies of the past twelve months' worth of checks."

"And if they decline to provide them?"

"We slap them with the warrant you will have arranged for in advance and we raid the joint."

Chapter Fifty-five

"You'll have to agree to their conditions," I said to Bob Albanis, who was currently in the George Murphy Detention Center, a mid-sized correctional facility located in the city of Maplewood.

"What conditions?"

"The usual."

"You'll have to forgive me if I don't exactly know what the usual conditions are for Witness Protection qualification."

He sat morosely, waiting for me to continue. When I didn't, he said, "You can't expect me to agree to something I know nothing about."

"I can if you want to save your ass. Once they realize their distribution network has been compromised, the Blackbirds are going to want to peck your eyes out. Worse, even."

"So what you're saying is I should sign anything the Feds put in front of me."

"I would."

"Without benefit of counsel."

"Listen up, Bob," I said. "Witness Protection is a very big deal. The Sheriff took some heat regarding this arrangement. There was a considerable amount of federal sentiment that you should face whatever music the Birds might choose to play for you. So, in other words, Bob, just sign the fucking documents and get the hell out of Dodge."

"Where will they take me?'

"Last I heard they were considering Aleppo."

"You're kidding, right?"

"Who, me?"

"Jesus, Steel. This is serious stuff to me. Quit pulling my chain."

"She'll be here sometime this afternoon."

"Who will?"

"Special Agent Eleanor Berezin. She'll see to the arrangements and make sure you're securely resettled. Wherever they place you.

"I guess the files helped."

"Tell me how they worked it."

"Who?"

"The Longs and the Dariens."

A slow grin began to illuminate Albanis' face.

"Some of what I believe is conjecture," he said.

"Okay."

"It started to go south about six months ago. That's when, to my way of thinking, the fail-safe line was breached."

"Meaning?"

"Until then, the reported rate of return on monies invested with investment brokerages like Darien's had pretty much leveled out at between four and five percent. Light years above the less than one percent the Feds were holding the line on.

"Suddenly, Darien's statements began showing returns of close to twelve percent. Which caught my attention. I began to have reservations about Mr. Oliver Darien. He smelled like Bernard Madoff. But when I relayed my suspicions to Hickey, he shut me down.

"He was always a stubborn fuck, Hickey was. Nobody could tell him anything. No one could disagree with him. Instead of being wary of Darien's twelve percent, he couldn't wait to tell the Birds and convince them to throw in with Darien, too. He was desperate to impress them. Told them it was foolproof. No risk. Scoop up the dough with both hands."

"And?"

"For the first few months, on paper, Darien appeared to deliver on his twelve percent promise. I'm guessing that resulted in a lot of fresh capital flowing into his coffers, capital he couldn't spread around fast enough. He believed he could fool all of the people all of the time. Then it went south.

"The statements kept coming but the cash didn't. Sensing something was seriously wrong, Hickey confronted Darien and demanded payment. The rest is history."

"And you were privy to it."

"I knew it was too good to be true, but Hickey refused to believe me when I told him. When you're raking in that kind of dough, it's tough to look it in the eye."

"I have one last question for you."

"You can have as many as you want."

"Something's been keeping me awake. I haven't been able to put my finger on it. So tell me, it was a setup, right?"

"What was?"

"The night we broke into your private little sanctuary at Long Pavilion?"

"What are you talking about?"

"What were you doing there? Ten o'clock at night. In rolled-up shirtsleeves and your desk littered with papers and file folders. And your feigned surprise and consternation. It was a setup. You had already duplicated and hidden everything. Your exit card was ready to be punched. All you needed was an opportunity. When we invaded the Pavilion, you saw it. You raced downstairs ahead of us and sat waiting for us to break down the door."

"You have a rich imagination, Mr. Steel."

"But I'm right, aren't I?"

"I have no idea what you're talking about."

"You don't how lucky you are, Albanis. A bit of advice, though. Keep your nose clean wherever the Feds put you. Don't fuck it up. You get caught doing anything even the slightest bit nutty and they'll cut you loose in a New York minute."

I turned away from him and headed for the door.

He called out to me. "What, no thank you?"

I stopped and turned back to him. "For what?"

"My help in proving your case."

"You go have a nice life, Bob. Courtesy of the taxpayers. That's your thank you. But I keep having this nagging feeling that you may be too smart for your own good. That you're destined to fuck up again. Try not to prove me right."

Chapter Fifty-six

"I'll need to have them processed," District Attorney Michael Lytell said, indicating the files and the spreadsheets that sat on his desk.

We were in his glass-walled office, overlooking much of San Remo County as well as a section of the California coastline.

My father, in full regalia, medals and all, sat in the leather armchair across from Lytell. Skip Wilder and I sat crowded together on a two-seater sofa.

Shifting awkwardly to face him, I asked the DA, "How long will it take?"

"A while. Paperwork like this needs to be carefully evaluated. Why?"

"Because if it's going to go on for any length of time, I propose we take him into custody straight away. And hold him without bail. Once he knows we're making him for the drug business, he's a flight risk."

"He's old. He's broke," Lytell said. "And besides, where's he gonna go?"

"Somewhere. Anywhere. What difference does it make? But you can be certain that wherever he goes, the shit's gonna come flying into your face for having granted him bail."

"Your kid has some mouth on him, Burton," Lytell said to my father.

"He's right, Mike," the Sheriff said. "Hold him. Judge Azenberg will issue the order."

"Barry Kornbluth will have a conniption."

"Barry Kornbluth should be worried about disbarment," I said. "He's played real loose with the facts of this case."

"He's not going to be disbarred," Lytell insisted.

"Ah," I said, "of course he's not. How stupid of me. For a moment there, I almost forgot about the San Remo old boys' network."

"There is no San Remo old boys' network," Lytell stated defensively.

"Yeah, and someday chickens will grow teeth."

Lytell looked at my father. "What did I tell you?"

"I think we should get on with this," ADA Skip Wilder said. "What do you want to do about arresting Senior?"

Lytell sighed. "What do you think, Burt?" he asked my father.

"I say we arrest."

"Skip?"

"I agree with Burton."

After a while, Lytell sank back into his chair. "Okay. My office will prepare the paperwork."

We all stood.

"This poor son of a bitch has lost everything," Lytell muttered. "First his money. Now his freedom. I feel sorry for him. It's a very sad story."

"Feeding addictive narcotics to children is a sad story," I said. "Holding a lowlife dip shit accountable for his despicable behavior is called justice."

Chapter Fifty-seven

I had been parked in front of the house on Loretto Drive for over an hour. It was a refurbished Colonial, the columned front of which put me in mind of Leslie Howard's manse in *Gone With the Wind*.

It stood on nearly two acres of mountainous terrain, its foundation carved into a stretch of leveled expanse midway up the hillside. It was a massive structure, looming tall above the homes in the valley below. There was parking for what must have been twenty cars. The mansion's second-floor picture windows, with their white, slatted shutters, overlooked the Pacific. Further up the mountainside, a tiered area had been bulldozed to accommodate a swimming pool, and higher still, on yet another leveled tier, a tennis court.

I watched as the Prius hybrid made its way up Loretto, past where I was parked. It turned right at the front gate of the Colonial and began to climb the hill toward the big house. Suddenly it stopped and lingered on the driveway for several moments. Then it carefully executed a U-turn and came back down to Loretto. It turned left and pulled up behind my cruiser.

Margaret de Winter stepped out of the Prius. After a moment's hesitation, she headed in my direction. I was already out of the car when she reached me.

She was wearing snug-fitting jeans and a slate gray hoodie. Her auburn hair was tied in a ponytail, which emphasized her beautifully sculpted face. She wore no makeup.

"What are you doing here?"

"I wanted to see you."

"And you thought the most efficient way of doing that was to surveil my father's house?"

"Something like that."

"What is it, Buddy?"

I couldn't quite find the words I was seeking.

"Quit phumphering," she said. "What do you want?"

"Me, too," I said.

"You, too, what?"

"I think I love you."

A glut of emotional responses flashed rapidly across her face, then just as quickly vanished. "You think?"

"Okay. I know. I love you."

"There's another shoe that hasn't dropped yet, isn't there?"

"Can we at least take a moment to appreciate what I told you?"

"Sure." She stood quietly for a moment.

"Now, what *didn't* you tell me?"

I had difficulty finding the right words so I remained silent.

"This is turning bleaker by the moment," she said. "Tell me everything you came here to say or I'm getting back in my car."

Finally I spoke. "When I first met you, I was collecting information regarding your family."

"I remember."

"It wasn't my intention to fall in love with you."

"Ditto."

"I never meant to hurt you."

"Come on, Buddy, out with it."

"I shouldn't be talking to you about this."

"You're referring to your ethics?"

"Yes."

"This has something to do with my family?"

"It does."

"With my father?"

"And your brothers."

"Do you want to be more specific?"

"There's enough evidence to bring criminal charges against them."

"All of them?"

"I'm not certain about Barry, Junior."

"What will happen to them?"

"That will be up to the courts to decide. But the odds favor jail time. Likely for your father, and surely for Hickey, if he ever turns up."

She started to say something but thought better of it. She turned as if to walk away but thought better of that, too. She glared at me.

I lowered my eyes. "I'm sorry, Maggie. This isn't how I wanted things to be."

"What about Barry?"

"The Reverend?"

"Yes."

"Uncertain. My guess would be no jail time. Probation, maybe. Public service. Again, it's not really my table."

"So it's your plan to bring down my entire family."

"It isn't a plan."

"But when we met, you were veering in that direction."

"They're not innocents, Maggie. They did manage to break several laws which, by the way, I took an oath to uphold. Narcotics trafficking. Tax evasion. Murder. Take your pick. I'm here because I didn't want you to be blindsided."

She reached down and scooped up a handful of pebbles that she proceeded to toss one at a time into the weeds by the side of the road. "You have to do what you have to do, Buddy."

When she finished tossing the stones, she looked at me for several moments. "I realize these bozos are out of control. They were sleazeballs to begin with and then they got taken to the cleaners."

She struggled to find the right words. "I lived with my head in the sand, Buddy. I took their money and looked the other way. For what it's worth, I'm hunting for a different direction."

She looked down and kicked at a few random stones in the road. "It's so ironic when you think about it. You wander around, always expecting that one day you'll meet someone who counts. You look high and low. You try not to lose hope. Then one day, there he is. You know it in an instant. You lose whatever control you may have thought you had over your emotions. You blindly jump with both feet and pray you land safely. Then life rises up and bites you in the ass."

She walked to her car, and once there, looked back at me. "It could never have worked between us."

She shook her head once, climbed into the Prius and drove away.

Chapter Fifty-eight

Barry Long, Senior, looked up when Johnny Kennerly and I entered his office. A frown creased his forehead. "What do you two bozos want?"

"I have to ask you to come with us," I said.

"Why?"

"I have a warrant for your arrest." Johnny stepped over to him and cuffed him.

"Now wait just a minute," Long said. "I want to exercise my right to phone my lawyer."

"That'll have to wait until you get to the station," Kennerly said.

"Like hell, it'll have to wait." He tried to kick Johnny in the leg but he evaded it. "Do you know who I am?" Senior Long huffed.

"I know who you were," I said. "Who you are now has yet to be determined."

● ● ● ● ●

The bank had provided enough signed checks to confirm Barry Long, Senior's involvement in the illicit drug operation. I was amazed at how cavalier he had been. He assumed that by destroying his files, he would walk free.

He never surmised he would be sabotaged from within. It was his trusted CPA who toppled his house of cards. It was his friend, Oliver Darien, who decimated it.

"Birds of a feather," I mused.

I drove up the winding driveway and was greeted in the motor court by Barry Long, Junior. Instead of being surrounded by a cadre of thugs, he was accompanied only by his wife, Catharine, and his son, Barry Three.

When I got out of the cruiser, the Reverend approached and extended his hand. "Welcome."

I didn't accept his handshake. "Thank you for seeing me."

I nodded to Catharine, who held my gaze.

"Come in," Barry said.

He, Catharine, and I trailed after Three, who had raced ahead of us, bounding onto the porch and into the house, allowing the big screen door to slam shut behind him.

"Five-year-old energy," the Reverend said. "Totally exhausting."

Catharine called out to someone named Esperanza, who then appeared with Barry Three in tow.

"*Esta bien,*" Esperanza said.

Catharine nodded.

The front hallway and the living room beyond were filled with cardboard boxes, all of them labeled, all bulging at the seams. Everything else had been removed. The walls were bare. Tables stood absent the lamps or tchotchkes that had adorned them.

As the Reverend led us to his study, he commented, "We're moving out this weekend."

The study had likewise been rendered bare. A few chairs remained, but most everything else had been packed up and loaded out.

The three of us sat.

"I'd offer you something," Catharine said. "But I have nothing left to offer."

I nodded.

"We realized we'd have to turn the house over to whomever the court-appointed conservator might be. So we figured, why wait?"

"For the District Attorney's directive, for one thing," I said.

"We've spoken with Mr. Lytell and have assured him that, although we intend to leave Freedom, we will keep him apprised as to our whereabouts."

"Hopefully, you'll do a better job of it than you did earlier regarding Catharine's whereabouts."

The Reverend moved quickly away from having to deal with that statement. "Mr. Lytell confided that he has no immediate plans to indict us."

Then, with a quick glance at Catharine, he said, "I meant to say he has no plans to indict me."

Catharine's attentions were tightly focused on her husband. I stared at her for a few moments, then turned back to the Reverend. "So you have no remorse, is that the case?"

"Regarding?"

"Everything that happened. Keeping your wife imprisoned, for openers."

"It was a mistake," he said.

"A mistake?"

"I made any number of errors in judgment, Sheriff Steel. The first was ceding so much authority over my affairs to my father and brother. I had no idea they were engaged in any criminal activities."

"Which still doesn't excuse your complicity with regard to Catharine's imprisonment."

"I came to realize that, but too late."

Once again he shot a glance at his wife. "Catharine learned before I did about the dire state of our finances. She confronted Hickey. They argued. She threatened to contact the authorities. Hickey had already placed her in the cell by the time I found out."

"And you did nothing about it."

"I told you I made judgment errors. That was one of them."

"But none of that makes you any less accountable for your actions."

"I see that now."

We sat quietly for a while.

Emboldened by the silence, the Reverend spoke out with a great deal of self-assurance. "I've emerged from this a better man. Catharine stands beside me. My son is with me. It's true I lost my fortune, but I regained my faith. I still have the ear of God, who has forgiven me. And my dedication to helping the poor and unfortunate has been renewed and strengthened."

Catherine flashed Barry a look of abject disgust. She got up from her chair and stood over him. "You know something, Barry," she snarled, "you are totally full of shit."

Jolted, the Reverend faced her, concern spreading over his upturned face.

"You and your self-righteous father and your deplorable brother. You're all full of shit. You're nothing but a trio of inept con men. And for your information, I don't stand beside you. I'm not like your sister. The truth is, you sicken me."

She looked toward the door. Jeffrey Bruce, the former intern, had wandered in and was leaning against it. She turned back to the Reverend. "It's over, Barry," she said.

A thin sheen of perspiration had appeared on his forehead. "What are you talking about? Why is he here?"

"The Barry Long, Junior, show has closed," Catharine said. "I'm running it now. Tomorrow's *Los Angeles Times* will exclusively headline the story of how you and your family kidnapped me and held me captive. And on Friday, I'll be Katie Couric's only guest."

Jeffrey meandered over to Catharine and rested his hand on her shoulder. She smiled at him and turned back to the Reverend.

"Did you know that Jeffrey here has a new calling?"

Barry stared at her blank-eyed. She went on. "He's joined the Noble Agency, and will be representing me and packaging my TV show, which, by the way, will be syndicated both domestically and abroad.

"Three and I will be appearing together and we plan to deliver a powerful message of hope and redemption to those who once had faith in you. Just like I did. But it's my show now, Barry, and it's sure to be a huge success. Thanks to my agent here, I'll be extremely well compensated for it."

Jeffrey grinned then flashed the Reverend a disparaging glance.

Catharine railed on. "While you and your family are defending yourselves against the criminal lawsuit I'll be slapping you with, my son and I will be raising our voices in praise of a God who saw fit to release us from your oppression. Who gave me the courage to stand up for my own rights and to also act as a spokesperson for the rights of women everywhere."

"Worldwide," Jeffrey added.

"Oh, and Barry," Catharine said, "just FYI, I filed for divorce this morning. No more community property, in case you thought you'd be sharing in the proceeds."

The full weight of all this had begun to register with Reverend Barry. "Catharine, Catharine," he pleaded. "Can't we at least talk this over?"

Catharine reached back and delivered a roundhouse blow to the Reverend's face. He recoiled and grabbed his cheek.

"Do you have any idea what it's like to be held captive, Barry? Against your will? Scared out of your wits?"

All sad-eyed and contrite, Barry whined, "I told you how much I regretted that, Catharine. I thought you had forgiven me. That we were still a family."

"You're toast, Barry. And just when things were going so well for you."

She picked up her bag and gave me one last glance. She and Jeffrey headed for the door.

Then she stopped to glare at Reverend Barry once again. "In case you're interested, the show is titled, *Rise Up.*"

Chapter Fifty-nine

The first few drops of a misting rain began to fall as I exited the Ralphs and headed for my cruiser.

Ralphs was the largest supermarket in Freedom, yet on this particular Sunday morning, the parking lot was mostly empty. I had stocked up for the week and as I loaded my two shopping bags into the backseat, I noticed that the egg carton, which had been carefully placed at the top of one of the bags, was dripping. When I opened it, I spotted two cracked eggs.

"Shit," I muttered.

I picked up the dripping carton, and had begun berating myself for not having checked it before leaving the market, when I became aware of Hickham Long, standing beside the car parked adjacent to mine, pointing a Glock .22 semi-automatic pistol at me. He had a look of self-satisfaction on his lopsided face.

"Well, well, well," he said. "Would you looky here. Is this an incredible coincidence or what?"

"Are you done?"

"Done? I haven't even started."

"Do me a favor, Hickey. If you're planning to shoot me, just do it and spare me the sound of your voice."

"A smart ass to the end. It's amazing how difficult you made things for us."

"What's amazing is how difficult you made things for yourself."

"That's one way of looking at it."

"It's the only way of looking at it. Put the gun down, Hickey. Turn yourself in."

"Not likely."

"What did you do with the money?"

"What money?"

"Surely you can lie better than that. Where is it?"

Hickey glared at me but didn't speak.

"I'm guessing you settled up with the Blackbirds," I said. "Took the heat off of your old man. Anything to win his approval. Isn't that right, Hickey? Daddy's devoted son."

"Shut up, asshole."

"Actually it's Sheriff Asshole. You're done, Hickey. Time to cash out."

The rain began to fall in earnest, soaking us both.

"And if I did?"

"You'd probably pull a lifer."

"I'd probably pull a lethal."

"Not likely. Not in California. The bleeding heart liberals out here hate lethals. You're more likely to live to a ripe old age in a snazzy San Quentin guest dwelling. Big screen TV. En suite bath and shower. Room service. Hell, you might even make someone a lovely wife. Livin' it up at the Hotel California."

"That's enough of your horse shit. Is this your way of begging for your life?"

"Not hardly. I don't really give a rat's ass about my life. You want to take it, be my guest."

"You're so full of shit, you know that?"

I realized I was still holding the egg carton.

"Just so you know," I said. "I'm going to put this egg carton inside my car. If you want to shoot me, please feel free to do so."

Hickey grinned and moved in front of the car he had been standing beside. He took a couple of steps in my direction, keeping his gun trained on me all the while.

I showed him the carton and slowly walked toward the rear of the cruiser. With my back turned, he wasn't in a position to see me grab hold of a pair of eggs. He was totally flummoxed when I whirled and threw both of them at his head.

The first one struck him in the right eye, the second on the chin. Pieces of shattered shell and gooey egg drippings splattered his face. Startled, he moved to defend himself, but I was on him before he could.

I grabbed his wrist with my left hand and, with my right, grabbed the gun barrel and jammed it into his mid-section. I let go of the barrel and took hold of his index finger, which was still on the trigger of the Glock.

He attempted to wrestle the pistol free, turning his hip as if readying to drop me.

But his eyes registered horror when he suddenly realized I was jamming his trigger finger with my own. Without warning, his stomach was blasted by a .40 mm cartridge that blew a hole in his mid-section the size of a small picture window.

The astonished look in his eyes quickly faded to blank. I stepped away as he collapsed into a newly formed puddle on the rain-swept parking lot, his dead face disfigured by the splatter of egg yolks and large shell chips.

I knelt beside his fallen body and checked for signs of life. There were none. I stood up slowly and examined myself for any gunshot residue. Aside from a few blood splashes, I was okay. I opened the trunk of the cruiser and removed the tarp I kept there. I covered the body with it, shook off the rain, and climbed into the cruiser where I sat silently for several minutes.

Then I punched the number of the station into my cell phone and when Marsha Russo answered, I told her what had gone down.

"You okay?"

"A little wet is all."

"That's not what I meant."

"It boiled down to him or me. I offered him an out. He refused to take it."

"Are you going to start beating yourself up now?"

"I don't know, Marsha. I killed a man. If I look closely enough, I'm fairly certain I'll spot a way it could have been avoided."

"Don't second guess yourself, Buddy. It was the right thing to do."

"If you say so."

"I say so. The Blackbirds will be happy. You did their job for them."

"It's not over with the Blackbirds."

"Meaning?"

"There's a day of reckoning in store for them. I've got a new mantra.

"Which is?"

"No gangs in Dodge."

"The Birds aren't going to like that mantra."

"You think?"

"I do."

"Isn't that a crying shame?"

Chapter Sixty

"He suffered a stroke," my father said.

"Who did?"

"Who do you think?"

"Long Senior?

The old man nodded.

We were seated in my condo where he had come to visit after checking out the site of the Hickham Long shooting. His condition had stabilized for the moment and his spirits were high. He showed flashes of his normally cryptic self, which pleased him.

He wandered idly around the condo, looking into each of the rooms. "I still can't understand why you chose this over the mansion."

"Privacy."

"Privacy's overrated. Life's comforts and a handful of servants trump privacy any day."

"He's still alive, I gather."

"The doctors say he'll survive."

"Big surprise," I said. "Any complications?"

"Only for the District Attorney."

My father sat heavily on one of my armchairs. "He's not a young man and if there are physical consequences as a result of the stroke, they'll make prosecution problematic."

"So he'll walk free."

"If he's able to walk."

"You don't really believe this stroke nonsense, do you?"

"What I believe is irrelevant. If the doctors say he's impaired in any way, the DA will be forced to take that into consideration."

"What was it the DA said? *This is a sad story*, right?"

"Yes."

"Even sadder now that Hickey's gone."

"Yes."

"Barry Long, Senior, is a crook. A con man. Been one all his life. He trained both of his boys to walk in his footsteps. The irony is how he fell prey to someone else's con."

After a while, my father said, "They'll never prosecute."

"Why not?"

"The Lytell factor. He'll stick to his sad story thesis. He sees Senior Long as Job. He lost everything, and if that weren't enough, he now has to deal with the anguish caused by the death of his eldest son. Plus, he's had a stroke. Could things be any worse?"

"Hook, line, and sinker," I said.

"What's that supposed to mean?"

"This entire thesis is a bucket of con-artist crap. The old man didn't think Hickey could be counted on to bail him out so he suffered a so-called stroke. He knew Hickey was a cartel target and feared they would not only put the exclamation point on Hickey's life story, but conceivably on his as well. So he gambled the cartel wouldn't come after a dying man. Hence the stroke. Which proved irrelevant because the devoted son had already ridden to his rescue."

"And died in the process."

"But not at the hands of the cartel."

My father shifted in his seat. He appeared to be experiencing some difficulty breathing. When he saw me staring at him, he waved me off. "I'm fine."

I watched him closely, all the while taking note of his physical condition. "Hickey could have taken the Darien dough and gone into hiding with it," I told him. "Good-bye and good luck. Instead, he used it to vindicate his father, who will no doubt surprise everyone by experiencing a miraculous recovery. A sad story, my ass."

"Are you suggesting that Hickey took one for the team?"

"I am."

"Why would he do that?"

"Because he had to know they'd never let him walk away. Despite the return of the money, the score was still unsettled and one of them had to pay the price for it. So Hickey set out to martyr himself. But first he chose to settle accounts with me, following which his plan was to cough himself up to the cartel. What better way to look good in his old man's eyes than by erasing me, and then taking a bullet himself?"

"Who cares?" the Sheriff said. "One less scumbag for the State to house and feed."

"Compassion becomes you."

"Fuck compassion. It's better for us this way. It's off our plate."

My father wrestled himself to his feet. "Politically speaking, you're the big winner here, Buddy."

"Politically speaking?"

"That's right."

"It's funny, you know."

"What is?"

"I had my reservations about coming back here. I like L.A. I like being part of the LAPD culture. Their politics are firmly rooted in irony. You win some, you lose some. And sometimes the ones you win are a whole lot worse than the ones you lose. When I came back to Freedom, I had hopes that small-town politics were more honorable."

"And?"

"They're less so. They're encased in psychological corruption—based on the misguided belief that the ways and means of a small town are superior to those of a big city. Which is a crock of hypocritical bullshit."

"You're a cynical man, Buddy."

"You think?"

When he reached the door, he turned to me. "You play your cards right and this business with the Longs could well prove to be your ticket to a brilliant future. Your name on any ballot will promise a near-certain winner."

"The only win for me is doing well what you asked me here to do. The father and son stuff. It's why I came and it's why I'll stay. This is about us, Burton. Nothing else."

"It heartens me to hear you say that, Buddy."

We looked at each other.

"I meant it when I said you could have a large future here," my father said. "It's a place where you could make a difference. You're a winner here. Despite your cynicism. The choice is yours."

He closed the door softly behind him.

"Some fucking choice," I said to the door.

Chapter Sixty-one

It took a while to find her. She had moved from the Los Feliz Towers leaving no forwarding address.

I surmised that out of all of her options, Vegas was the likeliest. Work was readily available. One could live quietly in near-anonymity. I took the chance she was there.

After turning up nothing but blanks, I was able to convince the Las Vegas Sheriff's Department to allow me access to their digital files of hotel employment applications for the past several months. Law enforcement regulations called for background checks on any potential gaming industry employee.

It was the name Margaret Short on a recent job application that caught my attention. Margaret Short had been hired by the Wynn organization and was working as a cocktail waitress at the Encore.

I planted myself in front of the employee entrance, watching the midnight shift-change when I spotted her. She exited in the company of two other women. Once outside, they said their good nights and headed off in opposite directions.

She walked away with her head down. I fell into step behind her. Sensing she was being followed, she wheeled around. She had lost weight. Her face looked gaunt. Her hair was cut short.

When she saw it was me, she stood staring as if frozen to the spot. Then she stepped up to me and slapped me hard in the face.

"For Hickey?"

"For Hickey."

"Would it help if I told you I had no choice?"

"No. And I should probably do it again.

"For Catharine?"

"Of course, for Catharine. Her TV show is a hit and the two Barrys are dead broke."

"Perhaps there's a God after all."

"Must you always be so cynical?"

"I had nothing to do with it."

"Oh, please. You had everything to do with it."

"It was Catharine's eleventh hour surprise. You have to hand it to her. She suckered the Reverend and he never saw it coming. What is it they say about a dish served cold?"

The desert winds had turned brisk. She shivered visibly. "I waited for you, Buddy."

She moved close and put her arms around me. She held tight, trembling slightly, her face buried in my shoulder. She leaned back, tears now in the corners of her eyes, and caressed my cheek where she slapped me. She kissed me tentatively. "I wasn't sure you would find me. Or if you even wanted to find me."

"What are you doing here?"

"In Las Vegas?"

"Yes."

"If I tell you, will you think me an oddball?"

"It's possible."

She hesitated before answering. "Re-inventing myself."

"And?"

"I'm a work in progress."

I couldn't resist a smile. I pulled her close and kissed her. I slowly traced the curve of her lips with my finger. "Was there anything you wanted to know?"

She gazed into my eyes and whispered, "What took you so long?"

Author's Note

Please note that San Remo County and its cities, including Freedom, are fictional places. No such county or cities exist in the state of California.

Acknowledgments

Many thanks to…

…my friends at PPP…Barbara Peters, Annette Rogers, Michael Barson, Diane DiBiase, Beth Deveny, Raj Dayal, Holli Roach, and Robert Rosenwald…with gratitude for their support and encouragement;

…my extraordinary team of champions…Tom Distler, Melanie Mintz, Steven Brandman, Miles Brandman, Emanuel Azenberg, Steve Shepard, and Roy Gnan…

…my friend and partner, Tom Selleck…

…my mentors…Robert B. Parker, Elmore Leonard, Lee Rich, Ivan Held, Christine Pepe, Bruce Jay Friedman, Arthur Miller, and Tom Stoppard…

…and my great pal, Helen Brann, who meant the world to me…

To see more Poisoned Pen Press titles:

Visit our website:
poisonedpenpress.com/
Request a digital catalog:
info@poisonedpenpress.com